GAMES LOVERS PLAY

MERRY FARMER

OLIVER
HEBER
BOOKS

Copyright ©2021 by Merry Farmer

Published by Oliver-Heber Books

0 9 8 7 6 5 4 3 2 1

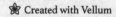 Created with Vellum

1

YORKSHIRE, NEAR HULL – JULY 1816

Every night, Redmond Wodehouse returned to the same, haunted place.

The sun beat down merrily on the deck of the HMS Majesty. Red strode from the fore to the aft, his hands behind his back, surveying the work of the Majesty's crew. The mood of the ship was tranquil, as they hadn't seen any sort of action at all for more than a fortnight. The American privateers they'd been chasing out of British waters surrounding Nova Scotia knew that the war was nearing its end as much as the British sailors knew it. Instead of cleaning the canons, checking stores of gunpowder, and polishing swords in preparation for action, the crew were scattered about the decks repairing sails, inspecting rope for weak points, or scrubbing the decking and rails to keep the ship in perfect shape.

Red smiled at the shanties a group of the Majesty's sailors with particularly melodious voices sang. A few men who should have been tending to their duties had brought out instruments—a fiddle, a flute, and a bodhran, in the case of Davy Kelley—but rather than scolding them for shirking their duties, Red let them play.

He let them play.

It was his watch, after all, which meant he made the rules and was responsible for everyone's actions. If Captain Wallace took umbrage with the lax behavior of the crew, Red would let himself be blamed for it. After all they'd been through, and knowing the war would be over soon, the crew deserved a few hours of peaceful enjoyment. Besides, the hornpipes that some of the sailors had started dancing on the starboard side of the main deck were energetic enough to build muscle and keep those sailors fit for action, if they saw any again.

"What-ho, Billy!" one of the midshipmen shouted from high overhead in the rigging. "Watch this!"

Red paused to glance above, raising a hand to shield his eyes. The scene unfolded in vivid, dream colors and sharpness. Overhead, Oliver—a spritely lad of fourteen who fancied himself the leader of the midshipmen, even though most of the lads were older than him—grabbed hold of a rope that hung loose from the fore topsail yard. He pushed off of the yard and flew through the air in a wide arc, landing deftly on the yard jutting out on the other side of the foremast with preternatural grace. His actions had an angelic, unreal feeling. The other midshipmen cheered him on.

"Careful there, Oliver," Red called up to him. "The rigging is for raising and lowering the sails, not turning midshipmen into monkeys."

"I saw a monkey once," Billy, the oldest of the midshipmen at age eighteen, called from the crow's nest. "When I was a cabin boy on a merchant ship that sailed to Bombay."

"I want to go to Bombay," Oliver called back to him, adjusting his grip on the rope. "When the war is over, I'm going to find a position on a merchant ship and sail the world."

"You're going to go home to your mama first, though, young man," Red told him with a laugh.

The other midshipmen laughed along with them from their various perches along the yardarms high above.

"I am not," Oliver argued with a peevish pout. "I'm not a baby anymore. I'm a grown man, and I intend to sail all the way around the world. Just you wait."

Red shook his head and continued his patrol, chuckling at the lad's enthusiasm as he did. He'd been that young and full of dreams once too. That was what had taken him out to sea in the first place and enabled him to show the heroism that ended up with him being granted an unlikely title, in spite of being the youngest son of a duke. As far as he was concerned, the title could go hang itself. A life at sea was the life for Red, just like it was for young Oliver.

He breathed in the salt air, letting it fill him with contentment. The gentle sound of the waves lapping at the Majesty's hull and the cries of sea birds above was as musical to him as the merry tune the sailors played. Indeed, the birds seemed to be singing along. Red reached the stairs leading up to the quarter deck and turned to make his way back to the fore, happier than he'd ever been. Peace was coming, things would be quiet, and if all went well, he could meet Luc ashore that night for a little fun.

His thoughts were shattered a moment later as three things happened in quick succession. The midshipmen above started shouting in alarm, the sea birds squawking along with them. A loud crack sounded. And young Oliver tumbled down through the rigging, dropping like a lead weight, and landing with a sickening crunch on the main deck several yards in front of Red. The lad's body splayed at unnatural angles, and he didn't move.

Red jerked forward, running to him, but everything slowed and warped. He couldn't move, couldn't cry out. The sky darkened and seemed to turn red at the edges. His

*arms and legs felt like they were made of slippery seaweed
that didn't work right. He couldn't reach Oliver. He couldn't
help him, couldn't save him. It was too late.*

It was all his fault.

RED AWOKE WITH A START, screaming into his pillow.
His bedcovers had managed to tangle themselves
around his legs, and his nightshirt had bunched
around his torso. It and the sheets under him were
drenched in sweat, as was Red's pillow. He stopped
screaming as soon as he awoke, but his lungs continued to burn as he gasped and wheezed for breath,
as if he'd been through a battle and barely escaped
with his life.

Sense snapped through Red like a whip's crack,
and he groaned and flopped to his back. A flood of
emotion threatened to pull him under as his eyes
stung with tears. He gulped a few more breaths,
flinging his arm over his eyes and willing himself not
to sob. More often than not, he lost that battle and
spent the greater part of the first fifteen minutes
after he woke from the nightmares every morning
sobbing like an infant as he remembered that afternoon.

It had been his watch. He should have told the
boys to stop messing about in the rigging. He should
have scolded Oliver Shaw for risking his neck by
showing off.

No, Shaw hadn't been showing off, he'd been
working.

Or perhaps he'd been tying something to the top
of the mast?

Every time Red had the dream, it was something
different, but the truth of the matter remained the

same. Shaw had fallen to his death, and it had been Red's fault.

He should have kept order, maintained discipline. Instead, a fourteen-year-old lad was dead, his dreams of sailing the world dead with him. So much potential, so much loss. And Shaw wasn't the only one. How many of his fellow sailors had been blown to smithereens or lost in a storm or succumbed to illness? And yet, he was spared. Why?

A sob made its way up from Red's lungs before he could stop it. The sound was loud enough to startle him and slap sense into him. Red moved his arm from his face and stared up at the cracked ceiling above him, willing his breathing to come more steadily. He wasn't on the *Majesty* anymore. He was home, at Wodehouse Abbey, and had been for more than a month now. He was no longer in charge of anyone, man or boy. He had no responsibilities, no duties. It was for the best. It was safer that way. But dammit, it was unfair.

He closed his eyes and scrubbed his hands over his face, brushing his damp hair back from his forehead. He kicked out of the sheets and bedcovers so that he could let his damp body dry in the early morning air. Above all, he continued to force himself to breath in long, steady breaths until he was calm. The navy was far behind him. He didn't have to set foot on a ship again for the rest of his life. As long as he was under his older brother, Anthony's, roof, he didn't have to make any decisions or take charge. All he had to do was continue to pretend nothing was wrong and he was his usual, jolly self. And best of all, Luc was coming today, at last.

Red let out a shaky breath and forced his mouth into a lascivious smile. Yes, that was what he needed.

The only reason the nightmares had been so bad of late was because he'd gone too long without a thorough tupping. He'd been as chaste as a monk since arriving at Wodehouse Abbey, and it was wearing on him. Especially since Anthony and his best friend, Barrett Landers, were now paramours, and Red and Barrett's other shipmate, Septimus Bolton, had taken Anthony's children's tutor, Adam Seymour, to his bed. Red was surrounded by men who were finding sexual satisfaction with each other on an almost hourly basis while he'd been celibate. That was the problem.

All that would change as soon as Luc and the other officers from the *HMS Hawk* arrived later that morning, as per the letter Lucas had sent a few days before. Red took a deep breath and rolled to the side, pushing out of bed entirely. He and Luc had developed an understanding almost from the moment they'd met. They'd liked the look of each other from the start, tiddled each other a bit after drinking too much rum, then swiftly fell into an arrangement where they would roger each other silly whenever they felt the need and duty allowed it. Luc certainly hadn't been the only willing partner Red had found in his seafaring days, but he was by far the best.

That was what he needed, he told himself as he stripped off his nightshirt, leaving it on the floor for the footman who was serving as his valet to pick up, and went to splash cold water from the basin on his washstand over his face and chest. He needed Luc's warm, solid body against his, Luc's mouth on his own or on his cock, and Luc's pert, round arse to bury himself in until they were both flush with pleasure and could find their release. Red scrubbed the sweat of his nightmare off his body, toweled himself dry, and took a razor to his face, convincing himself more and more that a bit of activity with Luc was all he needed to chase his demons away.

He did such a good job of convincing himself— truly, he did, absolutely—that by the time he was cleaned up, dressed, and on his way downstairs to the breakfast room, he had a smile on his face and a bit of bounce in his step. Never mind that his insides still felt like a mess of tangled and frayed ropes or the fact that he nearly jumped out of his skin when he stepped on a stair that creaked loudly. He would do what he'd done since first returning to his family home. He would pretend that he was happy, that didn't have a care in the world. He would pretend so hard that everyone around him would continue to believe it.

"Good Lord, Red," Anthony greeted him as he walked into the breakfast room. "Are you well? You look as though you wrestled the Devil last night and the Devil won."

Red's teeth were immediately on edge. "I'm perfectly fine," he said with a laugh, ambling over to clap a hand on his brother's shoulder before veering off to fix himself a plate of sausage and eggs to break his fast. "It's a beautiful day, Yorkshire has brought out its finest weather to entertain us, and the rest of our miscreant band of ex-officers will be here at any moment."

"Yes, I am most interested in meeting the rest of your friends," Lord Percival Montague, Baron Sigglesthorpe, commented from his place at the opposite end of the table. "I do love a naval officer," Percy added with a lascivious wiggle of one eyebrow.

Red laughed, more relieved by Percy's wicked observation than he could measure, as he brought his breakfast to the table and sat across from the man. "Percy, what are you still doing here?" he asked, sitting, then pulling his chair into the table. "You weren't invited in the first place." He winked as he reached for the teapot closest to his place.

"A good friend is always invited," Percy said with one of his usual, ridiculously affected off-hand gestures. "And I am far too entertaining to be given the heave-ho so soon after arriving."

"You arrived almost a fortnight ago," Anthony pointed out from the head of the table. He sent Barrett, who sat to his right around the corner, an overheated look, as though the two of them had discussed Percy's continued presence deep into the night, when they were deep into each other.

"A fortnight is no time at all," Percy said with an amiable smile.

Red was beyond glad that the ridiculous pouf was still with them. Percy was one of the most diverting men of Red's acquaintance. He was a dandy of the sort that would make Beau Brummel jealous. Even now, miles out into the middle of nowhere in Yorkshire, Percy was dressed in a peacock blue jacket and aubergine breeches, his hair was perfectly coifed, and his face was gently powdered. His lips were tinged dark pink, but whether that was from rouge or from having them around the cock of whatever footman, stableman, or farmer's son he had last gone to his knees for was anyone's guess. Percy was as degenerate as he was diverting, and Red loved him for it.

"Perhaps Anthony will sell you a portion of Wodehouse Abbey's estate so that you can build a house of your own here," Red teased him as he dove into his breakfast. "Seeing as everyone seems to be purchasing or selling land these days," he finished with his mouth full. Even the simple act of eating a well-prepared meal helped to banish the demons that had clawed at him just an hour before.

"Septimus and I are not purchasing the Henshaw house for our school," Adam spoke up from the end of the table, where he sat next to Septimus. "We're renting for now." The smile he sent Septimus and the corresponding look of adoration that Septimus gave him was so charming that it nearly turned Red's stomach.

"Perhaps someday we can purchase it outright," Septimus told Adam, resting his large, calloused hand over Adam's slender, soft one.

Red sent a look Barrett's way, intending to share a teasing glance with his best friend, but Barrett was already exchanging that sort of glance with Anthony. The two of them had fallen completely, madly in love in the last few weeks. Red was overjoyed for his brother—who hadn't had the slightest inkling that he fancied men until Barrett came along—and his friend, but their contentment with each other only stirred the unease roiling in Red's gut. Luc couldn't arrive soon enough.

"And what about this proposed land sale that Mr. Goddard has been so insistent about?" Red asked Anthony. He told himself he had not asked the question to bring an end to the banquet of love unfolding around the table, but not only did Anthony break away from gazing at Barrett as though Barrett had hung the moon, Adam made an impatient sound and stabbed one of the sausages on his plate. Mr. Martin Goddard—who worked for Hamilton, Bradley, and Associates as a land broker—was an old schoolmate and rival of Adam's. The two had had more than one unpleasant encounter that summer.

"What about the sale?" Anthony asked, returning his attention to Red while continuing to eat.

Red shrugged. "Are you going to follow through

with it? Is it really worth carving up an ancient estate and selling a slice to one of these mad industrialists? They seem to be cropping up all over England like weeds."

"Industry is profitable," Percy jumped into the conversation with a shrug. "All anyone in certain circles desires to talk of these days is steam engines and the uses to which they can be put. I've heard speculation that all of England will be dotted with steam-powered factories of one sort or another within a decade."

"Factories," Septimus snorted, shaking his head. "They're nothing but dirty heaps that squeeze the life out of good country folk."

"And make their owners into astoundingly wealthy men," Red pointed out, gesturing with his fork in Septimus's direction. "Why, I've heard of men in Lancashire who were born into poverty, but who could buy half the dukes in England five times over now." He turned his fork to Anthony with a wink.

He would have said more—and Anthony looked as though he would argue the point—but a commotion in the hall not only ended the conversation, it stopped Red's heart in his chest. He sat up straighter, dropping his fork and abandoning his breakfast, and strained his ears until he was certain the voices he heard coming from the front hall were those of his friends from the *Hawk*. Indeed, Clarence Bond's booming voice would be obvious even in the middle of a raging storm, but Red held his breath in the hope that he might hear Luc's voice as well.

"Looks like the rest of our motley gang has arrived at last," Barrett said, sending a knowing look down the table to Red.

Breakfast was abandoned as they all stood and made their way out to the hall.

"I'll just go up to the nursery and fetch the children," Adam said with a smile, striding off ahead of their group as they spilled into the hall. "I'm certain they'd enjoy meeting the new guests before their lessons."

Red could barely keep his excitement in check. He'd missed his friends. Clarence was always good for a laugh, and he'd been anxious to hear how Spencer was faring after the accident aboard the *Hawk* that had nearly blown his ear off. But as they made their way to the front of the house, where Mr. Worthington, the butler, was directing all four of Wodehouse Abbey's footmen in sorting baggage and taking the coats of the newcomers, Red only had eyes for Luc.

The moment Luc turned away from handing his coat and hat to Dan, the footman, and turned to meet Red's eyes, Red's heart felt as though it might burst in his chest. Luc looked well. He was tall and well-formed, with a square jaw and warm, brown eyes that glittered with mirth. His skin was still somewhat tanned, even though the delay that the *Hawk's* crew had experienced before making their way to Yorkshire had seen them waylaid in Portsmouth for weeks instead of out at sea. There were roses in Luc's cheeks, and his curling hair looked wind-tossed from the ride up from Hull, even though he'd worn a hat. In short, he was every bit as gorgeous as Red remembered him to be, and just the sight of him had Red's cock hardening in his breeches.

"Gentlemen, welcome," Anthony said, taking the lead, as was only right, considering he was a duke and Wodehouse Abbey was his house. He strode forward, taking Clarence's hand first. "I have heard so much about you all in the last few weeks that I feel as though we are friends already."

"Your Grace," Clarence said, bowing graciously. That alone was nearly enough to make Red snort with laughter. Clarence Bond was the least gracious, least refined man that Red had ever known. He laughed at what he called the ridiculousness of nobility most of the time, but he showed Anthony respect. It was only fitting, since Anthony was the one offering his own home as a place of respite for as long as Red's friends chose to stay there.

"I should make all of the introductions," Red said, dragging his eyes reluctantly away from Luc and stepping forward to Anthony's side.

"Yes, please do," Percy said in a salacious purr, sweeping Clarence with a hungry look, then moving that giddy, assessing perusal on to Spencer and Lucas.

Red sent Percy a sideways smirk before launching into introductions. "Gents," he told the men from the *Hawk* with utmost informality, "allow me to introduce my brother, Anthony Wodehouse, the Duke of Malton."

"It is a pleasure to have you here," Anthony said, shaking Spencer's then Luc's hands.

"I am grateful for your hospitality," Spencer replied, just a bit too loudly.

Red shifted to stand with the men from the *Hawk*. "This is Mr. Spencer Brightling," he explained for Anthony's and Percy's benefit.

"Mr. Brightling," Percy said in a purr, stepping forward to offer a hand daintily to Spencer, his hips cocked at a theatrical angle, as though he were trying to be as fey as possible. "The pleasure is all mine."

"I beg your pardon?" Spencer asked, again too loudly, looking utterly confused and embarrassed.

Clarence burst into loud laughter. "Aren't you a pretty penny," he said, nudging Spencer aside so he could take Percy's hand and kiss it, as though Percy was a debutante in her first season.

"Oh, my," Percy said breathlessly, batting his eyelashes up at Clarence.

Red rolled his eyes and sent Luc a look. He was rewarded deliciously when Luc returned that look with a knowing one, nearly laughing in the process. The connection between them was still there. In fact, it was as if the two of them hadn't spent any time apart at all. Red could have shouted for joy. At last, the nightmares would end and he could drown his sorrows in pleasure and amusement.

"And this is Mr. Lucas Salterford," Red said, using the introduction as an excuse to move to Luc's side. He caught a whiff of Luc's familiar scent. It was enough to send his blood roaring through him.

"Mr. Salterford." Anthony stepped away from the display that Percy was making of himself for Clarence and grasped Luc's hand.

"It is a pleasure to meet you at last, Lord Malton," Luc said with a smile.

"No, not Lord Malton," Red corrected him. "My lofty brother is a duke, so it is either just plain 'Malton' or 'Your Grace'."

"Oh." Luc blushed in embarrassment. It was so gorgeous that Red could barely contain himself.

"Just Anthony will do," Anthony said with an almost embarrassed look. "It isn't correct or proper, but if I've learned one thing this summer," he glanced fondly to Barrett, "it's that the usual rules of society should not apply among our particular kind of friends."

"Oh," Luc said with an entirely different intonation, his expression brightening in surprise.

"We have a great deal to catch up on," Red murmured to him.

"Yes, I can see that," Luc replied, leaning closer. He glanced between Anthony and Barrett, then sent Red a questioning look.

"And I am Lord Percival Alexander Ignatius Montague, Barron Sigglesthorpe," Percy burst in to introduce himself, making eyes at Clarence as he did. "But you can call my Percy. Or poppet, if you'd like." He hooked his arm through Clarence's and drew him off toward the closest parlor. "Allow me to give you a tour of this magnificent house and all of its treasures."

Anthony sent Barrett a look that said they would have a particular kind of trouble on their hands where Percy was concerned, if they weren't careful.

In Red's estimation, a tour of the house was precisely what he needed, particularly if it meant he could personally show Luc some of the hidden corners and secret nooks.

"A tour sounds magnificent," he said quickly, taking Luc's hand. "You simply must see the passageway that was used to hide royalists during the Civil War."

He started to pull Luc down the hall, but was stopped by Spencer's somewhat distressed, "I am terribly sorry, but I did not catch what was said. I've lost hearing in this ear," he touched his left ear, "and hearing on this side is somewhat diminished."

"We're giving tours of the house," Barrett told Spencer, speaking up without making a spectacle of himself or Spencer. "Come along. Anthony and I will show you around."

Spencer nodded, looking grateful and embarrassed at once, and followed Anthony and Barrett into the parlor where Red could hear Percy prattling on. Septimus went with them.

"Should we go?" Luc asked, moving as if he, too, would follow.

"We'll meet them in the gallery," Red said, tugging Luc down the hall to the hidden door under the stairs. "First, I want to show you this."

He unlatched the secret door and swung it open, then pulled Luc into the narrow and shadowy corridor behind it. They hurried along to a second door several yards down, which let out into a narrow, unfurnished room with a single, high window at the far end. The room had a history of secrets and scandal, so it was the perfect place for what Red had in mind.

Which meant it was the perfect place for Red to swing Luc around and shove his back up against the wall.

"I have missed you more than you can possibly know," he managed to breathe out before pressing himself into Luc and slanting his mouth over Luc's in a kiss that he had fantasized about for months.

2

Lucas Salterford's heart hadn't stopped pounding from the moment he spied the odd collection of towers, turrets, and gardens that made up the manor house of Wodehouse Abbey. Every mile he'd had to cross to make his way back to Red, every delay the *Hawk* and its crew had experienced, had been torture for him. He'd endured countless interviews with the Admiralty as his future was decided, suffered through a short, awkward reunion with his family in Portsmouth, and nearly bankrupted himself paying for passage—along with Spencer and Clarence—to Yorkshire. Through all that time, he'd dreamed of Red every night, dreamed of holding his sometimes-lover in his arms, kissing and caressing his powerful body, and finally summoning the courage to speak the words he'd never been able to utter before.

Now, here he was, alone with Red in a strange, secluded room that seemed perfectly designed for illicit trysts. His back pressed against the dusty panels of one wall, grinding one shoulder blade painfully, enough dust tickling his nose to have him in serious danger of sneezing, but he couldn't remember a time when he'd been happier.

Because at last, his arms were wrapped around Red, Red's heat and energy infused him, and after Red had murmured words Luc had waited so long to hear, their mouths had crashed together in a reunion that stole the breath from Luc's lungs.

"I missed you too," he barely managed to breathe out as Red's mouth mastered his.

Red merely growled in response and kissed him harder, fumbling with the buttons of Luc's jacket. It was heaven. Luc let Red ravish him, let Red's tongue invade his mouth and claim him. Usually, they switched off between who played the role of aggressor, depending on their moods, but at the moment, Luc wanted nothing more than to give himself over fully to Red's lusts. It had been so bloody long.

"I think we can dispense with this," Red gasped, lips swollen and pink, as he finished with the buttons of Luc's jacket and pushed it from his shoulders. "This too." He went to work unfastening Luc's waistcoat. The bottom button became caught somehow, which caused a frustrated growl from Red before he grabbed both sides of the garment and yanked so hard the button popped off.

Luc laughed. "It is fortunate that I do not care for clothing the way you do." He fussed with the buttons of Red's jacket as he spoke.

"I only care for your clothing when it lies in a crumpled ball on the floor beside my bed," Red laughed as well, then loosened Luc's breeches enough to tug his shirt up.

As soon as Luc's belly and chest were exposed, Red dove into him, sliding his hands along every inch of exposed flesh and bringing his mouth down over one of Luc's nipples. Luc groaned with pleasure, tipping his head back against the wall and closing his eyes for a moment so he could revel in the sensations.

So. Bloody. Long. He didn't care that he'd only just arrived at Wodehouse Abbey and that he had, in essence snubbed his host, Red's brother. He was utterly unconcerned with the way his and Red's friends would tease them mercilessly as soon as they emerged from their reunion. All he cared about was the throb in his prick as it responded eagerly to Red's every touch and kiss, and the corresponding ache in his heart.

He loved Red. Loved him more than sense, more than reason. He had almost from the first moment they'd met. Red was lively and intelligent, beautiful, and excessively talented in so many ways, as demonstrated by the way his tongue swirled around Luc's nipple before he kissed his way southward.

"I've been dreaming of this since we last parted," Luc gasped, threading his fingers through Red's silken hair as Red's mouth trailed lower. "I hate being apart from you. I don't ever want us to be parted for this long again. I—"

His long overdue confession was cut short as Red suddenly straightened and slammed his mouth over Luc's. Luc made a sound of utter surrender as Red sucked his tongue into his mouth. He still had his fingers threaded through Red's hair and pressed his fingertips into Red's scalp the way he knew his lover liked. The result was that both of them were left panting, groaning, and grasping at each other.

"God, how I wish I'd thought to carry lubrication with me today," Red panted between kisses, his hands reaching for the falls of Luc's breeches. "I would turn you around, rip your breeches down to expose that fine arse of yours, and fuck you until you painted the wall with your seed."

Luc made a half-mad sound of longing and launched himself against Red, pulling his shirt out of his breeches so that he could splay his hands along the bare skin of Red's torso. "And then I would return the favor," he purred, slipping his hands beneath Red's breeches to cup his arse. "I would return the favor a hundred times over."

"We could forget everything," Red sighed, then completely unfastened Luc's breeches so that he could scoop a hand in to draw out his cock. "We could forget everything but pleasure."

Luc was so aroused already that it took a supreme effort of will not to come in Red's hand, even though he supposed that was the point of Red's touch. He wanted the moment to last far longer than a few, desperate moments.

"I've spoken to the Admiralty," he panted between kisses, leaning his head back again and wishing he'd thought to untie his neckcloth so that Red could do more than nibble at the top of his neck. "I've asked to be assigned to a new ship, as captain, as soon as possible. The interviews were favorable, and there is a distinct possibility—"

"Shh," Red silenced him, punishing Luc's mouth with another wild kiss. "No Admiralty, no ships. Just this."

He drew his hand up the length of Luc's prick, pulling back his foreskin and brushing his thumb around his sensitive tip. Luc was already wet in anticipation, and Red spread the moisture in maddening circles over his slit that had him ready to come out of his skin with pleasure. When Luc moaned in response and leaned heavily against the wall, barely able to support his own weight, Red wrapped his hand carefully around Luc's shaft and worked him mercilessly.

"Good God," Luc gasped, rolling his head against the wall. He wanted to utter a string of obscenities to emphasize how good Red made him feel. He wanted to burst out with every confession of love that his heart had kept hidden for so long. Instead, he made an embarrassingly enthusiastic keening sound of pleasure as white-hot pleasure coursed through him. Seed erupted from him, spilling across Red's hand and the bits of his shirt that had bunched over his belly. Whether it was the length of time he'd gone without another man pleasuring him or his desperate joy at being with Red again, his orgasm seemed to go on and on, the aftershocks sending warm swirls of satisfaction through him.

"Beautiful as always," Red said, humor and desire in his voice. He released Luc's cock, briefly cleaned his hand on the hem of Luc's shirt, then undid the fastenings of his own breeches and took his prick out.

Luc didn't need instructions to know what to do. He'd anticipated that moment for so long that it felt perfect and inevitable for him to sink to his knees in front of Red. He'd missed the scent and taste of Red so much that he wasted no time closing his mouth around Red's cock and drawing him in as deeply as he could. Red moaned in appreciation and fisted one hand in Luc's hair.

Any other day, Luc would have taken his time, teasing and testing Red's patience. They would have laughed together as they tried to pleasure each other as much as possible without letting the other come. It was a game they'd formed through their years of dalliance, one that was immeasurably satisfying when played to win. But Luc's patience was already as thin as could be, and he could tell from the tension in Red's body that he was eager for release. So Luc gave it to him, sucking hard, using his hand on the base of Red's staff and his balls to speed things along, and stroking with his tongue until Red burst straight to the back of this throat with a guttural cry.

It was everything Luc had been missing and more. He swallowed, and when Red was done, he leaned back, resting against the wall for a moment, then slowly pushed himself to stand. Once he was upright, Red sagged against him, resting his forehead against the side of Luc's head as they paused to catch their breaths. Luc raised his arms to embrace Red, even though they were both overheated, reveling in the moment.

He could do it. He could say what he'd needed to say for too long. Now, in that moment of reunion and communion, he could whisper those three simple words that would open a whole new chapter in their lives, a chapter Luc had longed for. Now was the time.

"Red," he whispered, turning his head so that his lips brushed Red's ear. "I l—"

"Thank you," Red cut him off, pushing away from the wall and sending Luc a cheeky wink. "That's exactly what I've needed these past few weeks." He set to work straightening his clothes and refastening his breeches, failing to meet Luc's eyes. "You have no notion of what things have been like these past few weeks without anyone to fuck. Septimus was taken with my nephew and niece's tutor, Adam Seymour, right from the start, and then Barrett managed to convince my brother that he might like a good hard, cock up his arse now and then. The four of them have been like dogs in heat for more than a fortnight, and I've had no one with whom to relieve my suffering."

Luc finished catching his breath, his mouth hanging open in shock. He was certain Red didn't mean to be cruel, but the suggestion that their passionate reunion had been nothing more than a convenient release for him punctured his tender heart. A heart that now squeezed sharply with hurt.

He put on a rakish smile all the same and pushed away from the wall. "Glad I could be of service," he said as he went about tidying himself and refastening everything that had been undone or loosened. "Any time you want a bit of relief, I am, of course, yours."

"You've no idea how grateful I am for it," Red said, finishing with his own buttons, then reaching out to help Luc with his. There was a sudden heaviness to his expression that made Luc forget his own worries for the moment. "Convalescing at one's home after a war is all well and good, but it is much more pleasurable when one has one's particular friend on hand."

"And as I have just experienced, your hand is particularly pleasurable when it is on your friend," Luc said, falling into the playful banter that had always been a hallmark of his and Red's relationship. Red would be more likely to confess what was wrong if the mood remained light.

And something was most definitely wrong.

Red laughed, and when Luc's clothing was back in place, as though it had never been partially removed or mussed in the first place, he thumped Luc's arm, then nodded to a panel in the wall that looked somewhat different from the others. "Come on," he said. "I'll show you a shortcut we can use to rejoin the others."

He stepped away, pressing a spot on the wall that undid a latch of some sort. The wall swung open, and Red gestured for Luc to follow him through.

Luc cleared his throat—he could still taste Red on his tongue—and tugged his jacket, smoothed his hands over his breeches, and prayed that he didn't look as though he and Red had just thoroughly debauched each other as he walked through another small passageway.

That corridor ended with another hidden door that opened into what appeared to be a library or study of some sort. As he and Red entered the vast room from one end, Malton, Barrett, and the rest of their friends were just entering from the other. Luc's burning self-consciousness soared to towering heights when he saw there were two children with them.

"Uncle Red!" the girl, who looked to be about ten, called out. She rushed across the room to hug Red, but her eyes stayed fixed on Luc. "Papa says you've brought us another friend to play with."

Luc was suddenly aware of every tiny thing that might have given away the particular games he and Red had just been playing in the secret room. He was certain he was still flushed—as Red was—and that the scent of musk hung over him. It made the moment one of the most awkward of his life.

"I *have* brought you a new friend," Red said, pretending as though nothing at all were amiss. "Eliza, Francis," he said, addressing the girl and the boy who hurried over to join them, "this is my dear friend, Mr. Lucas Salterford. Luc, this is my niece, Lady Eliza, and my nephew, Lord Francis."

"How do you do?" Lady Eliza greeted Luc with a perfect curtsey.

"Were you on the *Majesty* too?" Lord Francis asked, cocking his head to one side.

"I served on the *Hawk*, my lord," Luc said, nodding respectfully to both children. They were mere babes, but they outranked him in all of the ways that society counted.

"Mr. Bond says that the *Hawk* was bigger than the *Majesty*," Lord Francis rushed on. "Is that true?"

Luc laughed, feeling slightly more at ease, seeing as neither the children nor the adults in the room seemed to be standing upon ceremony. "Both ships were of the same class," he explained. "Both were third rate ships of the line from the Royal Oak class, seventy-four guns, two decks, designed by Williams."

Lord Francis's eyes went wide. "Amazing," he said. "Mr. Seymour has been teaching us about the war, and Mr. Bolton all about ships, but I didn't think to ask him that."

"I should have taught you the classes of ships without being asked," Septimus commented from the other end of the room. Luc was struck by how fond he seemed to be of the children. He never would have pegged Septimus for one to like children, but when Lord Francis wandered back to his side, the two seemed quite taken with each other.

"We are partway through a tour of the house," Malton explained to Red with a poorly-concealed grin that said he knew precisely what Red and Luc had been up to. "Would you care to join us, or would you prefer to continue your own, private tour?"

Luc anticipated Red saying he wished to give him a private tour, and he was disappointed when he said, "We'll join you lot," with a contented smile. "The more the merrier."

Malton eyed him strangely for a moment, then said, "Very well, shall we?" He turned to Barrett, then glanced to the others.

The entire group moved sedately through the library as Lady Eliza took up a place near the front of the group and said, "The library holds more than a thousand books, and they are written in eight different languages, though most of them are in English. The oldest book in the collection dates from fifteen thirty-six, but I am not allowed to touch it."

Luc couldn't help but smile at the young lady and her expert knowledge of the house as they moved through it. Judging by the way Septimus's Mr. Seymour nodded encouragingly at the girl from time to time, Lady Eliza had been tutored in the ways of conducting a tour and in the knowledge of her family and her home.

Luc enjoyed listening to her, but he was relieved when Barrett subtly started walking by his side as they entered a long portrait gallery.

"I take it you had a pleasant reunion with Red?" he asked, sending Luc a cheeky, sideways grin.

Luc couldn't help but gloat and grin in reply. "It was everything I'd hoped for and more."

He and Barrett both chuckled as subtly as they could, given that all of their friends were around them. Red had gravitated toward his nephew and Septimus, but he sent Luc a slightly uncertain look when he heard the laughter. Luc met his gaze with a fond smile, but when Red instantly looked away, as though meeting each other's eyes was an accident, Luc's smile dropped.

"Oh dear," Barrett said, far too much teasing in his voice. "Do not tell me there is trouble between the two of you already."

"No trouble at all," Luc said with a shrug. "Red and I have only just been reunited. We have an understanding. We have always had an understanding. We provide each other with what we need."

Barrett made a scoffing noise and shook his head. "That is the biggest lie I've yet to hear," he said.

Luc sent his friend a sheepish smile. "Very well, then. I confess that I am hoping for more, now that the war is over and our lives are taking new shapes."

"Is that so?" Barrett still laughed at him, which did nothing to put Luc at ease.

When the others turned the corner at the end of the portrait gallery and walked on, Luc hung back with Barrett. As soon as he was satisfied that they were alone, Luc let out a breath and rubbed the back of his neck with a wince.

"I came here with the intention of being clear about my feelings toward Red," he told Barrett. "This dance of ours has gone on long enough. Surely, Red must know how I feel about him, how I have always felt."

"I am certain he does," Barrett agreed with a nod.

Luc was encouraged by that. "There you have it," he said. "As soon as I have the opportunity, I intend to confess my love for Red and to ask for his love in return."

Barrett's face pinching was the only reaction Luc got to his bold comment. It caused his confidence to waver.

"You do not think I should tell Red that I love him? That I have always loved him?" he asked.

"You misunderstand," Barrett rushed to say. "I most certainly do think you should reveal all to him." He paused, tilted his head to the side, then went on with, "But perhaps not immediately."

"Oh?" Luc's heart fluttered anxiously in his chest. "Why is that?"

Barrett let out a breath and smiled weakly at Luc. "The war is barely over," he said. "It was harder on some of us than others." He glanced to the doorway the others had crossed through.

Deep affection squeezed at Luc's heart. "Are you referring to the matter of Midshipman Shaw?"

"Among other things." Barrett nodded. "Red has been excessively jovial since returning to his family home. Too jovial. You and I both know the man uses good humor as a way to mask discomfort. I have no doubt that Red loves you as much as you love him, but I would advise you to ease into any declaration of love. Allow him to become used to you, used to having intimate company again."

"You think that will be enough to convince him to let his guard down?" Luc asked.

Barrett shrugged. "Perhaps. At the very least, it will allow him to remember how much he adores you. And who knows? Perhaps he will surprise you by declaring his love first."

He clapped a hand to Luc's shoulder, and the two of them moved on, slowly catching up with the others.

"I will take that advice," Luc said with a grateful smile.

There was only so long that he could wait for all of the matters of their hearts and bodies to sort themselves out, however. Unlike the others, his chances of finding a new ship were high. The Admiralty could send for him at any moment. But if they did, Luc fully intended to take Red with him on his next adventure.

3

———

The physical and mental relief that Red experienced with the arrival of Luc and the others was frighteningly short-lived. He was able to make it through the rest of the day with an easy disposition, laughing with his friends and catching up on everything they had endured in terms of naval bureaucracy during the process of the *Hawk* being decommissioned, and hearing about the short visits each man had made to their families—or in Spencer's case, physicians specializing in hearing loss. It was all pleasant and relaxing—particularly as the weather was fine and they could take tea in the garden—and in addition to the conversation, Percy was in rare form, flirting with all three of the newcomers.

Red told himself that he didn't mind the way Percy made eyes at Luc or touched his arm or hand now and then during the course of the afternoon's activity. Luc had every right to seek his pleasure wherever he wanted to find it, as did he. But Percy was cloying at times, and Red still felt as though he and Luc had unfinished business of an intimate nature, since their encounter in the secret room had been so brief.

He considered inviting Luc to share his bed that first night, but Luc deserved to situate himself in his own room without interference. Besides which, there were some things Red wasn't ready to share with even his deepest and most intimate friend—a fact which he remembered as he woke in the middle of the night, shouting as the nightmares struck him again. This time, Shaw had been pushed by one of the other midshipmen instead of swinging on the rope. Red wished to God he could remember what had actually happened that day, though he doubted it would settle him and banish his misery.

On top of all that, now that Luc was back by his side, particularly after the moments they'd stolen together, Red was left with the prickling feeling that a deeper current ran between him and Luc than he was prepared to face.

Taken all together, the nightmares and the lack of instant relief from his demons that he'd expected would come with Lucas's arrival had Red somewhat out of sorts the next morning as he made his way down to a considerably more crowded than usual breakfast room. He slipped into the room, hoping not to draw too much notice, but with the full complement of their circle of friends present, that was like begging for wind in the middle of a calm at sea.

"There he is at last," Clarence called out from his seat at the far end of the table, gesturing to Red with a piece of crisp bacon. "Did you have a good lie in?" he laughed.

"If I didn't know better," Septimus laughed, "I would think he was having a particular sort of lie in this morning. But Luc is right there, so that cannot be it."

The others laughed as well. Anthony looked mildly embarrassed to have such crude topics discussed at his breakfast table, but Percy seemed to react as though he'd found himself in some sort of Uranian heaven.

"I can assure you, it was nothing of the sort," Red said as he fixed himself a plate at the sideboard, then helped himself to a seat at the table at the corner on Anthony's left. "Because as you have observed, Luc is already halfway through his meal." He decided to play along with the bit of ribald fun the others were having, winking down the table at Luc as he took up his fork.

The mood continued to be light as the others laughed. Spencer leaned close to Clarence—likely to ask what had been said—then laughed a bit belatedly. Luc had returned Red's wink with a pink-cheeked smile, but the way he continued to study Red rather than eating his eggs sent an awkward quiver through Red. There was most definitely something there that felt heavy and serious, and at the moment, Red didn't think he could stomach anything more serious than what already haunted him.

"What sort of activities do you have planned for your guests today, Your Grace?" Clarence asked as he reached for a small pot of jam near the center of the table. "I have it on good authority that our convalescence this summer will be filled with every manner of delight." He winked at Percy for good measure.

Percy turned bright pink and shivered. Red wouldn't have been surprised if the peacock had come in his breeches at the look Clarence gave him.

"Barrett and I have devised every sort of game you could wish to play," he said, making his voice deliberately loud—both for Spencer's benefit and to drown out the quieter voices within him that whispered of fears he didn't want to think about.

"Be warned," Seymour said, one eyebrow arched. "The games those two have invented are brutal and violent." He said as much with a grin and a spark in his eyes.

"Violent?" Barrett balked, grinning as well. "I take offense at that, sir."

"You must admit that Septimus and Mr. Seymour nearly cracked each other's heads in that game several weeks ago," Red said.

"That was because they were suffering from an excess of pent-up lust and needed a way to expend it," Anthony said with surprising candor.

"And expend it we did," Septimus added with a wink for Seymour.

The rest of them, Red included, laughed raucously. A conversation such as that could only happen in a room of all male friends. It reminded Red so much of the ribald company and rude talk of men aboard a ship that, for the first time in a long time, he felt as though he were truly home.

That feeling was magnified when he glanced across the table to find Luc grinning at him. Red's heart seemed to both swell and settle in his chest, and for a moment, the lingering horror of his nightmares was banished.

Seymour blushed furiously at the teasing he had received. He cleared his throat and stood. "Gentlemen, if you will excuse me, my pupils await upstairs in the nursery."

"When do you plan to open this school you mentioned yesterday?" Spencer asked Septimus loudly as Seymour left the room.

"As soon as preparations are made," Septimus an-

swered. He nodded to the door Seymour had just left
through and went on with, "We've signed a lease on
the house. Next comes improvements to the house to
make it suitable for young boys to live in. Then we
search for staff, then pupils."

"It all sounds devilishly complicated," Clarence
said.

"I think it is a noble and good endeavor," Luc said.

"And what about you, Red?" Clarence asked. "Septimus has his tutor and his school, Barrett seems quite
occupied with his new position as Duchess of Malton." The others laughed. "What do you plan to do,
now that your commission is over?"

All eyes were suddenly on Red, but the only ones
that mattered were Luc's. Luc had a fond hopefulness
in his eyes that both warmed Red and made him
writhe. Their reunion the day before had been sweet
and passionate, but Red wasn't a fool. He'd heard what
Luc had started to say, what he hadn't allowed Luc to
say. The man had plans of his own, and he wanted
Red to be a part of them. Those plans involved the sea
and ships, though, and Red had no intention whatsoever of so much as looking at a ship again, if he could
help it.

He could not disappoint a man he cared for so
deeply, but more than that, he could not reconcile the
unfairness of a man like Luc caring for him when he
had done nothing to deserve it—nothing but surviving when so many other men had died.

Instead, he shrugged with feigned casualness and
grinned. "I have no need to do anything," he said. "I
am at the mercy of my brother, but he seems content
enough to care for me, indigent as I am."

The others laughed again. Red was encouraged by
their merriment.

"I intend to do nothing more than spending the summer playing wild, invented games and amusing myself in a variety of wicked ways," he continued. When he glanced down the table to Luc, Luc grinned and blushed. It was enough to make Red wish he could discover a way the two of them could play games with each other until they were both raw and sore.

"I, for one, am deeply curious as to what sort of games you *Majesty* lot have invented," Clarence said, pushing his plate back to indicate his breakfast was over. "And as soon as I learn them, I vow that I will thrash you all."

"Is that what you think?" Septimus asked, rising to the challenge.

"Old rivalries never truly die," Spencer laughed.

"Come on, then," Red said, taking one last bite of sausage, pushing his chair back, and standing. "Those games won't play themselves."

And the sooner he wore the rest of his friends out, the sooner he and Luc could find a quiet corner in which to bugger each other senseless. Maybe then the restlessness and anxiety in his soul would finally be doused.

Red was immediately proven wrong when Luc sent him an openly adoring look as he finished the last of his breakfast and stood as well. Everything about the man went straight to Red's heart, which was why he marched out of the room before Luc could come around the end of the table to walk by his side. Adoration was more than he deserved and more than he could face at the moment, even though it pained him to snub Luc. Everything in his life was pain now.

"Just you wait," he called over his shoulder to the others, feigning jollity and picking up his pace to keep

Luc from catching up to him. "The games Barrett and I have devised are all excessively diverting."

Luc didn't catch up to him as they made their way out to the back garden, but Barrett did.

"That was a bit rude, do you not think?" Barrett murmured to him as they cut across the yard to the chest of game implements that now lived permanently at the side of the trimmed lawn.

"I beg your pardon?" Red asked with a sinking feeling in his gut, affecting ignorance.

Barrett sent him a flat stare that said he knew everything that was going on. "Luc cares for you, Red. He's been trying to show it."

Red shrugged, though his back prickled with nerves. "Luc and I are friends," he insisted. "He's the best fuck I've ever had, and vice versa. We've kept each other satisfied all these years, but there's nothing more."

He couldn't look Barrett in the eye as he spoke, but fortunately, he didn't have to. They'd reached the chest, and he pulled open the top and began dragging out everything from pall-mall mallets to lawn bowling balls to stumps and bales.

"Which game are we playing?" Luc asked as he strode up to stand by Red's side, slightly behind him.

Red managed not to look pointedly at him and say, "Which indeed?" Instead, he thrust a mallet at Luc, grinned as though his very soul wasn't shredding itself to pieces with guilt and confusion, and said, "Why don't we make one up as we go along?"

More mallets were handed around to the others. Clarence, Spencer, and Luc—who had yet to experience any of the mad-capped games Red and Barrett had devised—took to the foolishness easily. Clarence was, of course, insistent that the men of the *Hawk* challenge the men of the *Majesty*. Percy declared that he was too finely dressed to soil himself and that he preferred to watch, which Red found perfectly believable. Anthony was more than happy to sit out as well, likely so that he could watch Barrett.

Three on a side was more than enough to invent a challenging game, and before long, Red was able to forget all of his troubles as he ran up and down the lawn, smacking balls with his mallet and deliberately ramming into his friends in an effort to knock them over.

Those efforts served their purpose when he toppled Luc ten minutes into the game and splayed himself atop him, pinning him with his hips.

"Not so quick to dash about the field now, are we?" he teased Luc, their faces only inches apart.

Luc laughed, relaxing his body in a way that had Red's tensing in delicious ways. "Now I understand your aim," he said, eyes dancing as he gazed up at Red. "You've invented these games for the expressed purpose of getting me under you."

"I don't need to invent a game for that," Red said with a wink. He rocked back to his knees, then offered Luc a hand to help him up.

The game continued, and as it did, the fire between Red and Luc slowly grew. It was precisely what Red needed. He dashed up and down the lawn, making up wild rules for the game that would take his mind farther from his troubles while feeding his baser instincts. He noted that he wasn't the only one flirting either. Percy had taken it upon himself to ply both Clarence and Spencer with refreshment that he'd procured from God only knew where every time there was a lull in the action. He tried flirting with Luc as well, but Red put a quick stop to that.

"I see what you're after," Percy whispered to Red as they all took a break to catch their breaths and enjoy refreshments in earnest. Red sent a questioning look to Percy, suddenly anxious that the man would think his affection for Luc was deeper than it was. Percy leaned closer to him and said, "I would not be averse to you and your friend sharing me, you know."

Red laughed out loud. Percy was joking, of course. At least, he desperately hoped so. It was just the sort of comment he needed to pull him out of his heavy thoughts once again.

A moment later, as the others lay down in the grass for a rest or sat in one of the chairs that the footmen had brought out, Luc inched his way over to Red. "What did Lord Sigglesthorpe say that had you laughing so hard?" he asked.

Red turned a teasing grin on Luc and said, "He offered to let you and I share him."

Luc was in the middle of gulping the punch that had been sent up for their refreshment and nearly choked on it. He coughed so hard that Red had to move behind him and thump his back. Luc doubled over to help clear his throat, and seeing as they'd all removed their jackets for the game, the position gave Red a fabulous view of Luc's bum that made him want to forego the game entirely.

He was still staring at Luc's arse when the odious Mr. Goddard and a grey-haired stranger were shown around the edge of the house by Worthington.

"Mr. Goddard and Mr. Haight, Your Grace," Worthington introduced them to Anthony, who stepped forward to play host.

Luc straightened, still coughing a bit, and swayed closer to Red. "Do you know them?" he croaked.

"I know Mr. Goddard somewhat," Red answered, eyes narrowed.

He didn't have time for any further explanation before Mr. Goddard advanced on Anthony, gesturing for the man with him to follow. "Your Grace," he began with barely a nod. Red narrowed his eyes. Goddard had the worst manners of nearly anyone he'd ever had the displeasure of meeting. "May I introduce you to Mr. Karl Haight," Goddard said, gesturing to the stranger, when he straightened. "Mr. Haight is the owner of Haight Industries. He is the factory owner interested in purchasing a parcel of your land."

"Good Lord," Red exclaimed, his brow shooting up. "The blighter has brought the wolf to our door."

Luc glanced from Red to Mr. Goddard and Mr. Haight with his own expression of surprise. "Your brother is planning to sell part of his estate?"

"Not exactly," Red said, his expression folding into a frown. "Mr. Goddard has been badgering Anthony about it, and my brother has yet to put his foot down and tell the blighter to go away."

"Mr. Haight, welcome to Wodehouse Abbey," Anthony greeted the newcomer with every bit of grace that had been bred into him by a long line of dukes.

"Thank you, Your Grace," Mr. Haight bowed respectfully to Anthony. "Please forgive me for this interruption. I insisted that Mr. Goddard had no need to bring me directly to the estate the moment I arrived in Yorkshire, but he seemed to think you would welcome our company."

Red caught the slightest hint of irritation in Anthony's eyes as he glanced to Goddard. He turned back to Haight with a smile and said, "Wodehouse Abbey will always open its doors for friends."

"It is generous of you to say so, Your Grace," Haight said with a smile.

"Perhaps now we can discuss the particulars of the land sale," Goddard said eagerly. "Acreage, for example and price per acre."

Luc's brow shot up even farther, and he turned to Red with a look of shock.

"We've been encountering this pest for weeks now," Red murmured behind his hand, using the moment as an excuse to lean closer to Luc. After a good half hour of exertion, Luc smelled masculine and enticing. "His greed is only outmatched by his sheer, mad determination to push Anthony into something I'm not convinced he wants."

"There is no need to rush these things." Haight was polite enough to look shocked by Goddard's mercenary insistence on talking business straight away. Red also noted that Haight's stance seemed to agree with his own feelings on the matter. "It appears we have interrupted the duke and his friends in the middle of some sort of sporting event."

"We've paused for refreshments," Anthony told the man with a smile, as if he'd decided Haight was better than the company he kept. "Please do join us."

Barrett and the others got up from their lounging positions and tugged at their clothing to make themselves somewhat more presentable. As there were no ladies present, they could get away with not donning their jackets, but most of them refastened the buttons of their waistcoats. Barrett was quick to take a seat by Anthony's side and showed particular interest as deeper introductions were made.

Luc sighed and clapped a hand on Red's shoulder. "I suppose that is the end of our games for today," he said wistfully.

The heaps of affection in Luc's expression tugged at Red's heart, but also ignited that part of him that wanted to run from what he didn't deserve. Or, if not run, then transform the deeper implications of affection back into raw lust.

"Nonsense," he said, moving away from the more serious assembly that was starting at the top of the lawn so that he could gather discarded mallets and balls.

Luc hurried after him, picking up articles of the game as well. "Does your brother not need you to help with his negotiations?" he asked.

Red shrugged as he carried an armful of things to the chest. "I doubt he does. He has Barrett to advise him these days, and to be honest, I find Goddard to be the most odious person in Yorkshire."

Luc laughed, then glanced anxiously over his shoulder as walked with Red. "Your brother won't divide the estate, will he?"

"No," Red said, reaching the chest and lifting the lid with one toe.

Inwardly, he wondered. Anthony had not rejected the potential sale outright when Goddard had first mentioned it. He wanted to investigate whether building a factory on the property would provide jobs and good fortune for the tenants and others in the area. The whole thing filled Red with the same sort of anxious fear and resistance to change that all serious matters raised in him.

"If you're certain His Grace will not need your assistance," Luc went on, dumping his armful of wickets into the chest, then straightening and fixing Red with a wicked grin, "then whatever shall you do with yourself this afternoon?"

The heat and invitation in Luc's smile was precisely the balm Red's soul needed. "I think a swim is in order," he said, adding a wink to his words so that Luc would know a swim wasn't all he had in mind.

"Do you propose we venture down to the seaside?" Luc asked.

"Not at all," Red said, grasping Luc's hand. "I have a much better idea."

4

L uc knew full well he and Red were sneaking away from the serious, civilized discussion between Malton and Mr. Haight on a matter of grave importance to all members of the Wodehouse family for the sole purpose of utterly misbehaving in a way that would shock most people. He knew that Red was avoiding the business of his family's estate for some reason, and that he was avoiding the likely tumultuous emotions that events aboard the *Majesty* several months ago had caused.

He knew, but with the prospect of being naked and sweaty in Red's arms within mere minutes, he had an extraordinarily difficult time convincing himself to care.

For the moment.

"Where are you taking me?" he asked Red in an amorous purr as the two of them made their way down the slope of the lawn toward what appeared to be a lake of some sort beside a small wood.

"To a clandestine pleasure garden that has been in use by the more scandalous members of the Wodehouse family for generations," Red replied, glancing to Luc with flushed cheeks and mischief in his eyes.

There was something more to his look that worried Luc, though. Underneath the desire and the playfulness that defined Red lay something tighter, something painful. Luc could feel it, but he was at a loss as to how he might draw it out so the two of them could face it together.

"I cannot wait," he said instead, walking closer to Red so that their fingers brushed.

That simple touch was magical. Red sent Luc another look redolent with lust, then grasped Luc's hand and darted forward.

They ran the rest of the way to the lake. Luc's heart was light, even as his mind whispered they were running away from matters that needed to be dealt with. He argued back to that voice, insisting that all troubles would be easier to face once he and Red were both thoroughly satisfied and limp in the afterglow of pleasure. Besides which, other than their tryst in the secret room the morning before, it had been nearly six months since Luc had given in to the throes of passion, and he was randier than a satyr.

"I take it we're going for a swim?" he asked as they approached a small jetty that stretched out toward the clear, blue-green water of the lake.

"We are," Red confirmed with a nod, pulling Luc past the jetty and along a small path that disappeared into the thick trees. "But I know of a better spot where we can drop anchor."

"I am breathless with anticipation," Luc laughed.

Red glanced fetchingly over his shoulder as they started down the path. "I would wager you are," he said with a flicker of one eyebrow.

The clandestine pleasure garden Red had mentioned turned out to be more of a reality than a jest. Roughly halfway around the lake, well-hidden in a stand of towering oaks and bordered by neatly-trimmed hedges was an attractive terrace. Whereas the rest of the wood seemed deliberately wild and untamed, the terrace was an oasis of sophistication. Its flagstones were neatly arranged and had soaked up a good deal of the morning sun. They were warm under Luc's feet as he and Red removed their boots and stockings, then set to work shedding the rest of their clothes.

The terrace held two rattan chairs, a table constructed of the same materials, and a wide chaise with a layer of cushions that, to Luc's dirty mind, seemed purposely designed for wickedness. A large chest sat at the end of the chaise, and Luc could only guess at its contents.

Instead of making use of the chaise immediately as they shed their clothes, however, Red marched to the jetty at the end of the terrace and dove into the lake. Luc decided that beginning with a swim was a sound idea after all and followed Red into the water.

"Such a perfectly-placed lake cannot possibly be a natural feature of the land," he commented as he and Red swam out toward the center of the cool water.

"You are correct," Red laughed as he stopped his swimming to tread water in the sunlight. "One of my ancestors or another expanded a modest pond that was a natural feature. Right about the time he crafted that wood. He was ahead of his time, the old bastard. Artificial wild places and ruins did not become popular until decades after he made these improvements."

"Then why did he create this lovely paradise?" Luc asked, swimming closer to Red. He wanted to slide his body against Red's and taste the water on his skin, but the lake was too deep to stand where they were, and without the constant motion of treading water, they would sink.

Red laughed again. "To seduce women, of course. Or perhaps a few men here and there. The family records are woefully silent on the issue of whether Anthony and I are the first of our line to fancy a nice, solid prick, or if others had the inclination but did not admit to it."

"I'm certain you are not the first," Luc grinned and swam in a circle around Red. "I once patronized a physician who swore the inclination of one man to make love to another was as natural as any congress between a man and a woman."

"Truly?" Red's brow lifted in surprise.

"Yes, but he was considered a quack and condemned by the church," Luc admitted with a chuckle. "But you know how things were in the Navy." He shrugged, since that was the only explanation needed.

Instead of laughing and mentioning one of the many stories of their exploits on shore leave or Red's tales from the *Majesty* or Luc's from the *Hawk*, Red grew suddenly melancholy. He leaned into the water and started to swim back to the shore, turning his back on Luc.

Luc winced, then started after him. It appeared his guess as to Red still being tied in Gordian knots over the events surrounding Midshipman Shaw was correct. Perhaps to the degree where it had spoiled the rest of their decidedly adventurous time in the Navy.

He put his theory to the test as soon as they climbed onto the jetty and made their way back to the warm stones of the terrace.

"I'm happy to be going back, you know," he said as he caught a towel that Red had retrieved from the chest near the chaise and tossed to him. "I expressed as much in the interview I had with the Admiralty about captaining a new ship. Our superiors were pleased with my enthusiasm. I expect to be contacted with orders within a fortnight, a month at the most."

Red laughed humorlessly. "Do not tell that to Septimus. He would likely expire with jealousy, since a captaincy was all he wanted for years."

Luc finished toweling himself, tilting his head to one side, then lowered himself to lie on the warm flagstones. It felt divine. "Septimus seems quite taken with his Mr. Seymour, though," he said. The thought of that, combined with the particular angle at which he glanced up at Red's naked, glistening body had his cock stirring.

"He is, the poor devil," Red said, swiping his towel over his body, then moving to lie on the stones by Luc's side. "I am alarmed at what has come over Septimus, Barrett, and my brother, where this horrific need to shackle themselves to another is concerned."

Luc lost his smile, and his budding erection flagged. He was certain Red didn't mean his words as a slight. They'd never once discussed their views on long-lasting relationships among their sort, though the poorly-kept secret was that they were as prevalent and satisfying as those between men and women. Perhaps happier, since such unions did not solidify fortunes, determine social positions, or forge alliances. As tempted as Luc was to see Red's statement as a rejection, he instinctively felt it was more of a deflection from things Red did not want to think about.

All the same, knowing that didn't stop Luc from twisting his head to look at Red lying beside him and saying, "I want you to come with me."

Red visibly tensed, in spite of the relaxing qualities of the warm flagstones. "I beg your pardon?" he asked, sending Luc a furtive glance before deliberately looking at the treetops above them.

Luc rolled to his side and propped his head on one arm, in spite of the discomfort of the stone against his elbow and hip. What was a little discomfort when the desires of his heart and the rest of his life were up for discussion? "I want you to come with me," he repeated. "The Admiralty will let me choose my lieutenants and first mate. From a list of their own, mind you," he added. "But you are on that list."

Red's tension remained rigidly in place, even though he laughed and rolled to face Luc. "I am hardly your first, mate," he joked.

Luc laughed, but he did not feel the mirth behind it. "I am serious, Redmond," he said, using his full name to emphasize as much. "I want you with me. Always. Imagine the perfection of the two of us serving on a ship together for a change instead of two—"

He got no further than that. Red pounced on him, pushing him to his back and straddling his hips. He planted his hands on either side of Luc and leaned down to capture his mouth in a searing kiss. It was an obvious diversionary tactic, it was more than a bit uncomfortable with the flagstones underneath them instead of a bed, and the lingering worry that someone might wander by and spot them hung at the back of Luc's mind, but that didn't stop his heart from singing or his cock from leaping to attention at the prospect of everything it had gone without for so long. He moaned into Red's mouth as their lips and tongues mated, sliding his hands up Red's thighs to grip two firm handfuls of his lovers arse, spreading his cheeks.

"Too long," Red panted as he broke away from Luc's mouth to lick the water from Luc's jaw and neck. "Much, much too long."

Red reached between them, grasping their pricks together and stroking. Luc groaned an expletive and arched into the touch, encouraging Red. They needed to discuss so many things. Red's hurt was palpable, and Luc was certain he was one of the only men who could resolve it. He knew full well he was being used as a distraction. But it had been too bloody long.

"The chaise," Red panted, lifting to all fours above Luc and nodding to the appealingly soft piece of furniture. "And I have a surprise for you in that chest."

The lascivious gleam in Red's eyes was enough to cause Luc to scramble out from under him and lunge for the chaise. It could wait. Everything they needed to talk about could wait. Red leapt up and moved toward the chest as Luc tumbled onto the deliciously soft cushion, then pulled out a small jar that had Luc ready to shout for joy.

"Clandestine pleasure garden indeed," he gasped, letting his legs fall open. He reached his arms over his head to grasp the top of the chaise as he did.

"Now there's a sight I would sail the seven seas to catch just a small glimpse of," Red said in a passion-deepened voice, drinking in the picture Luc made. He opened the jar and scooped some of its contents, spreading it over his already leaking cock while biting his lip.

Luc wasn't the only one who was a sight to behold. Just watching Red handle himself, his eyes flashing with lust, his body still damp from their swim, his cock thick and hard and slick, had Luc throbbing with need.

"I've waited months for this," he growled, letting go of the chaise with one hand so that he could stroke himself while Red watched him.

"So have I," Red said, kneeling on the cushions between Luc's knees. "I need you more than you can possibly know."

Red's words were arousing and beautiful, but Luc heard the desperation in them as well. He knew Red well enough to know exactly what the man was doing. He knew enough that he should have put a stop to their games until everything was sorted.

But when Red ordered, "Turn around and show me that delicious arse," Luc jumped to obey.

The chaise was, indeed, designed perfectly for fucking. The back was at exactly the right height and angle for him to lean against and grab hold of as Red shifted up behind him, parted his arse cheeks, and sunk the hot spear of his cock deep inside of him. Luc let out a groan of utter bliss, alternately relaxing so Red could press deeper and tensing so that he could feel every inch of him, the burn and the fullness. After a few exploratory thrusts to get his bearings, Red grabbed hold of Luc's hips, moving fast and hard, and causing both of them to make sounds that would startle the wildlife for miles around.

It was quick, it was crude, and it was everything Luc had needed for far too long. He gave himself over completely, his body singing with pleasure as Red used him. When Red leaned forward to bite his neck where it met his shoulder, Luc nearly came from the sweet possessiveness of the gesture. He held off, though, moving into Red and grasping Red's hand when it moved around to splay across his chest.

"Red," he panted as lightning began to coalesce near the base of his spine. "Red. I...I—"

His efforts to confess love were thwarted again as Red closed his free hand around Luc's iron-hard cock and stroked until Luc burst for him. It was so good that the edges of Luc's vision went white, and if not for

Red's arms around him and his body inside of him, he would have fallen over.

Red came a moment later, spilling himself with a grunt and a few final thrusts that slowed in intensity until he slipped out. The two of them collapsed onto the chaise in a messy pile of overheated, sweaty limbs, entwined with each other even though they were no longer joined.

"That was magnificent," Red panted, making a show of himself as he splayed.

He was the most beautiful thing Luc had ever seen. Luc took a moment to just study him, study the lean lines of Red's torso, the powerful muscles of his thighs, and the endless allure of his slick, flagging cock as it settled. Red always had been a work of art, but Luc found him priceless when he was glowing with satisfaction in the wake of a thoroughly good fuck. Best of all, every bit of the tension that had gripped him earlier had drained away. Perhaps now they could talk.

Sentimental as it was, Luc wriggled until he and Red were cuddled together, like two schoolgirls giggling over secrets in the tall grass of the fields near his home in Cumberland. He threw an arm and a leg over Red and nuzzled his neck for good measure, drinking in the scent of him—sweat, musk, sun, and lake water.

"I hated being apart from you," he confessed, eyes closed, drowsiness descending on him. "Even when we were aboard ship, I hated being apart from you."

"And I you," Red said in an equally sleepy voice.

Luc opened one eye and lifted himself just enough to peek at Red. Red had his eyes closed, and his face was soft with satisfaction. He must have meant what he'd said about hating the two of them being parted, because there was no artifice or avoidance in his expression.

"There is no rule that says we must live out the rest of our lives separated from each other, you know," he pointed out softly.

"None at all," Red agreed. He dropped a hand lazily to the inside of Luc's thigh and stroked his fingertips in a way that sent shivers through Luc.

Hope throbbed in Luc's heart. "We could spend our whole lives sailing together on one ship or another. We could go to the South Seas, to Cathay, to uncharted waters. We could—"

"I'm not going back to sea, Lucas." Red tensed all over again, opening his eyes and staring hard at Luc.

Luc held his breath for a moment, praying that he'd misheard. Then he let that breath out. He rested a hand over Red's heart, threading his fingers through the hair on Red's chest, and said, "It's because of what happened to Shaw, isn't it?"

Every part of Red went rock hard with tension. "I have no wish to discuss the matter," he said with brittle formality, confirming Luc's suspicions.

"The fault was not yours, Red." Luc lifted himself to one arm so that he could gaze down at Red. "Those boys were taking risks they knew they shouldn't have. None of you knew the rigging wasn't tied properly. Shaw was always so sure-footed. I'm certain he—"

"It was my watch." Red sat up abruptly, swinging his legs over the side of the chaise. "I was responsible for the boys. I was responsible for the rigging. I let my guard down, and now a boy is dead. It was all my doing."

Luc's heart tore within him as he shifted to sit behind Red, slipping his arms around him and holding him close in comfort. "Accidents happen, Red. It wasn't—"

"Did we come down here to talk of death and shame or did we come here to fuck?" Red cut him off more abruptly than ever, twisting to face Luc.

For a moment, Luc's mouth worked fruitlessly. He couldn't form a single one of his swirling thoughts into words. Red needed him, that much was obvious. He needed him in order to come to terms with what had happened and to let the demons of the past go. But it was as clear as the crystal sky above them that things were still too raw and brittle for Red to trust him that way.

Luc gave up with a sigh. "We came down here to fuck," he admitted. It felt like a horrible defeat.

"Then take that ointment, slick that gorgeous cock of yours, and stuff me like a cannon about to fire on a French frigate," he said with hollow teasing in his expression.

Luc held perfectly still, studying Red while his heart bled within him. He loved the man to distraction. All he wanted was for Red to feel whole and strong again. He was also just a man—a man finally reunited with his lover after months, and who was in as much need of physical satisfaction as Red was.

"Alright," he said with a salacious wink. "Show me that fine arse of yours and I'll help you imitate a cannon. I'll even get you to fire off."

Red laughed. It was an eerie sound that had the hair on the back of Luc's neck standing up. Fucking wasn't a solution to the problem, but if it would bring him closer to Red, he would tumble gladly with him. But they could not avoid the sea of troubles that surrounded them forever.

5

Having Luc at Wodehouse Abbey was supposed to relieve Red of the guilt and fears that haunted him, not create more of them. Luc was his friend and his coconspirator in countless games and antics of the past. The light rapport that the two of them had always enjoyed—not to mention the bone-melting pleasure the two seemed uniquely suited to give each other—should have served its purpose as just the thing Red needed to forget his troubles and return to the way things used to be.

But when he awoke from yet another nightmare—in which this time, he watched Shaw fall from the rigging because of a vicious gust of wind—he began to question whether Luc was truly the balm that his soul needed.

"Are you certain you've no wish to pay a call on Dr. Norris in Hull?" Anthony asked him quietly after their expanded company had finished breakfast and begun to disburse to their various activities for the day.

Red caught sight of Luc lingering near the doorway to the breakfast room, watching him with a look that resembled a puppy in fear of being left behind by his master, as he and Anthony headed toward

Anthony's study at the end of the hall. His heart clenched and twisted in his chest, giving off too many emotions for Red to keep track of.

"I am perfectly well, Tony," Red told his brother in a falsely cheerful voice as they veered into the study. Luc was still watching, and Red half believed he would attempt to intrude on the conversation he and Anthony were about to have. "I am in no need of a physician."

Anthony strode to his desk, but turned back to Red before he sat to go over the estate business for the day. "Are you quite certain? Because convalescence is meant to improve one's overall health after the horrors of war. You've grown thinner and paler with each week that has passed, and for the last sennight, the circles under your eyes have grown pronounced." He paused, his mouth tipping into a salacious smirk, then added, "Barrett seemed to think that Mr. Salterford's arrival would bring you relief. Is that not the case?"

Red swallowed hard, then force himself to a carefree smile. "Luc has provided a great deal of relief already," he replied with perhaps a bit too much cockiness. "And I have relieved him more than a few times in the days since his arrival as well."

Anthony turned bright pink and made a sound of embarrassed humor. That turned Red's own smile more genuine. His brother was endearing. Just because Anthony had uncovered the truth of his own nature that summer, after years of denying the truth, just because he'd found happiness and satisfaction with Barrett, it didn't mean he was not still reduced to blushes and giddy stammering when faced with the topic.

"As long as you are well in body, mind, and spirit, I will be happy," Anthony said, moving to sit at his desk.

The sentiment was kind, but Red's gut clenched all the same. Well in mind and spirit? Red dreaded to think what that comment was for. He'd done so well at concealing his inner turmoil from his brother for the past several weeks. Had Barrett gone and revealed all to him, the bastard?

"I should go," Red said, turning away from Anthony's desk. "Games do not invent themselves, after all. Leisure is exceedingly hard work."

Anthony laughed as he picked up a letter that lay open on his desktop. "Pray do not overexert yourself, brother," he said.

Red forced a laugh as he left the study. Anthony couldn't know the truth. He and Barrett had knit their souls together in no time at all, but Barrett had been Red's friend first. He would not whisper in Anthony's ear, like a debutante gossiping, and betray Red's trust. Besides, if Anthony knew about Oliver Shaw, he would have been disgusted by Red's incompetence and thrown him out of the house weeks ago.

Those thoughts were cut short as Red took two steps down the hall and nearly ran headlong into Luc. He gasped and reeled back, then cursed himself for being so startled when he knew full well Luc would be waiting for him. The man had hardly left him alone since arriving four days ago. Granted, Red had hardly left Luc alone either, but that didn't mean he wasn't startled.

"I have prepared a surprise for you," Luc said with a bright, teasing look in his eyes.

Red put on the sort of wide, devilish grin Luc likely expected of him, leaned closer to brush his fingertips against Luc's cheek, and said, "Is it a surprise that involves your bared arse lifted up and spread for me?"

Luc laughed and blushed. A twang hit Red's heart, gut, and cock that was both wonderful and deeply alarming.

"No, it's nothing like that," Luc laughed, filling Red with paradoxical relief. Luc's grin remained impish, though. "Perhaps later," he purred.

That, too, came as a relief to Red. He needed Luc.

No, he *wanted* Luc. That was all. He wanted to bury himself in Luc's strong, hard body. He wanted to be possessed by Luc as well. The need was only skin deep, though. Bedsport was the perfect way to push all bad thoughts aside, lock them up, and throw away the key. Not that he had let Luc anywhere near his actual bed. That would never happen as long as the nightmares persisted.

"What is this surprise that does not involved arses, then?" he asked, walking down the hall when Luc gestured for him to follow.

The answer came in the unlikely form of the youngest of Anthony's footmen standing near the front door with a small hamper. He handed the hamper off to Luc once he and Red reached the door, then bowed nicely and went about his work for the day. Red arched one eyebrow at the hamper in question.

"I've had your brother's cook provide us with a small luncheon that we can take to the beach," Luc said with an even wickeder grin than before.

"So it's to be a day by the beach, since you cannot and will not ever convince me to go back to sea?" Red asked as they headed out into the sunny morning.

Red noted the way Luc's teasing grin fell flat when he issued his subtle ultimatum. Red knew the man well enough to know when he was disappointed. And because Luc was his friend—his friend *only*—that disappointment settled like a burr in Red's chest.

"I thought we might walk down to see this house Septimus and his tutor have contracted to let for their school," Luc said, regaining his cheer as their feet crunched on the gravel of the Abbey's front drive. "Septimus informs me that there is an abandoned smuggler's cave farther along the beach as well that bears exploration."

"I know that cave well," Red said, some of his buoyancy returning. It would be enjoyable to show Luc the cave and all its wonders. "Anthony, George, and I used to play in there as boys," he went on as they strolled, maintaining a companionably close proximity. "Well, Anthony and George played. I was considerably younger than the two of them, and for a time, I was more of a nuisance to them than not."

"George is your other brother?" Luc asked as they walked.

Red hummed and nodded. "He and his wife, Marie, live closer to Whitby. George doesn't have a title—and he is excessively jealous of the one I earned in the war, I might add—but Marie was an only child, and as her father adored George, he left every bit of his extensive, profitable property to George, via Marie, when he passed."

It was an immeasurable relief to prattle on about land and its yields, tenants and their problems, and George and Marie's children as Red and Luc walked the mile and a half to the shore. Sex wasn't the only way a man could forget all of his problems. Miring himself in the domestic minutia of daily life was just as effective a distraction. It was a shame that his meager title hadn't come with land to match it. He intended to find himself some one day, but at the moment, he could only distract himself with other people's petty concerns.

Even those concerns were not enough. Not when they reached the beige ribbon of sand that ran along the coast, kissing the frothy waves that beat against Yorkshire from the North Sea, and Luc hinted at the true purpose of their outing.

"I never considered the coast of Yorkshire as beautiful," Luc said once they'd removed their boots and stockings so that they could walk toward the cave and the Henshaw house with their toes in the sand. "But I suppose anyplace can be considered beautiful when one is with the right company."

He edged closer to Red as they walked. Their arms brushed. Luc's fingers reached for Red's own.

Red's heart squeezed and ached in his chest. He veered away from Luc by a few inches, but couldn't maintain the distance for long. That rebellious traitor, his body, wanted to be up against Luc at all times, and that fool, his heart, shouted encouragement. But his mind warned against entanglements that he did not deserve, entanglements that would only lead to more innocent people being hurt.

He cared too much for Luc to let the man hurt himself by developing feelings Red could not reciprocate.

Only when Luc spoke again did Red realize that he'd let far too long of an awkward silence come between them. "You see?" Luc grinned at him. "The sea is not all bad."

"It is beautiful," Red admitted, feigning casualness when his insides felt as though they were splintering. "From this vantage point," he added.

Luc hesitated for so long Red's back began to itch

before saying, "This angle has its charms as well." He stared right at Red and not the sea as he spoke.

Red laughed as though Luc were teasing. "If you think that, then you are blind. Why, just this morning, Anthony was telling me that I look infinitely worse for wear instead of well-rested since returning to Wodehouse Abbey."

Again, Luc's expression not only fell flat, it pinched with concern. Deep concern. The sort of concern that came with other emotions that Red wanted nothing to do with.

Luc opened his mouth, but the only thing that came out was a half-formed syllable that didn't develop into anything. He kept his mouth open for a moment—Red forced himself into the obligatory thoughts that, with a shape like that, Luc's mouth belonged around his cock, but even that, ribald thought felt pale and forced—then shut it. He cleared his throat.

"Since you were raised on these shores, what is the best spot for us to unpack this hamper and see what Mrs. Abbott prepared for us?" he asked, his features softening into playfulness once more.

"We've only just broken our fast," Red pointed out. He picked up his pace and said, "Besides, the smugglers cave is right there, up ahead. I'll race you to it."

More than just his tense muscles groaned in relief as he broke into a run, dashing away from Luc and closer to the water so that he could run faster on the wet sand. His mind was pathetically grateful to have something else to concern itself with besides memories and emotions that were best left untouched. Running, racing, and climbing once he reached the jumble of rocks jutting out from the shore that had formed the smuggler's cave were precisely what he needed to distract himself with.

Red was even more grateful when Luc set the hamper against the wall of the cave and joined him in a competition to see who could climb to the top fastest. Luc's competitive streak was a godsend, and for a moment, Red thought it might have spared him the agony of discussing things.

He was proven wrong when the two of them made it to the jagged rocks at the top of the cave and found comfortable spots to sit while catching their breath. Luc blindsided him by blurting out, "It wouldn't be that bad, you know. I have every confidence that once you have your feet firmly planted on the deck of a ship-of-the-line, all of the turmoil that was caused by the accident will melt away."

Red's smile hardened into a grimace. "I am not going back to sea, Lucas," he growled, searching around him for a way to climb back down to the beach, even though he had yet to catch his breath from the climb up. That was half his problem. He'd never had time to catch his breath.

"I would be with you, Red." Luc scooted closer to him over the sharp rocks. "I know that your mind is troubled by Shaw's death, but I would be there. I will always be there for you, you know that, don't you?"

"We should climb down before whatever delights Cook made for us spoil," Red mumbled, deliberately not looking Luc in the eyes as he picked his way over the rocks to the point where they met the field at the top of the cliff.

"Redmond," Luc called after him, his voice tight with frustration. "This is not good for you."

"I know not of what you speak," Red said, falling

back into formality, though he wasn't certain he spoke loud enough for Luc to hear him.

"I think you do," Luc said, proving Red had spoken loud enough after all. "I think you've known how I feel for quite some time."

Red's face flared hot. He picked up his pace, stretching to scramble across the rocks with less care than he should have shown so that he could put as much distance between himself and Luc as possible.

Luc tried to keep up at first, but he must have sensed his cause was pointless. Instead of following Red all the way to the edge of the cliff and the field, he climbed back down the rocks to the beach to fetch the hamper and their boots and stockings.

"Will you at least make your way back down here so that we can eat?" Luc called up to him once they were both on level ground. "There's no need to discuss anything right now. We have the summer, and even though I expect to hear from the Admiralty soon, they may not require my answer immediately."

"I have no desire to go back to sea," Red called down, walking as close to the edge of the cliff as he dared while Luc followed on the beach below. Red almost grinned at how ridiculous Luc looked trying to carry a hamper and two pairs of boots and stockings while simultaneously walking fast enough to keep up with him. It was enough to prompt Red to slow his pace.

"I must respect your wishes not to take another commission," Luc continued while walking. "But there are other matters we should discuss as well. Important matters. Matters of the heart." He lowered his voice on that final sentence, almost as if he was too preemptively disappointed by how that conversation would progress to speak up.

Red's heart twisted and burned in his chest. He was not only an incompetent murderer of children and a bastard who did not deserve his own luck, he was the slayer of a good man's heart. It ate him up from the inside.

"There is a staircase up ahead," he called down, ignoring what Luc had just said. "You can come up that way and we'll eat our luncheon up here."

Luc nodded and headed toward the stairs. Once he'd joined Red on the top of the cliff, they did their best to brush their feet and legs free of sand, put on their stockings and boots, and move to find the most advantageous spot to sit and eat the feast Mrs. Abbott had provided. Blessedly, Luc didn't attempt to start any sort of discussion that Red had no wish to be a part of. Perhaps the man had a streak of self-preservation after all.

"Cook was generous with these meat pies," Red said with false cheer once they were seated with the picnic spread between them. "I'd wager I can eat two of them before you finish one."

Luc laughed, then said, "Never."

Within moments, the storm had cleared and Red felt as though he were on safe ground again. He and Luc laughed and made fools of themselves as they stuffed their faces with the meat pies. Mrs. Abbott had included bottles of ale as well, which were quite useful for washing down flakes of pastry and banishing bad feelings.

Simply eating the pies was not enough, though. Once Red's initial hunger was sated, and when it looked as though Luc might actually beat him in the contest, he smashed the remnants of his second pie against Luc's cheek instead of attempting to eat it. That led to Luc nearly choking with laughter in response, then throwing the last of his second pie at Red as well.

The picnic descended into a battle where the weapons of choice were hurled bits of food from the hamper, and that devolved into a wrestling match. When wrestling ended with Luc on his back while Red straddled him, pinning Luc's hands above his head, and Luc's body suddenly going slack in submission, Red couldn't help but dip down to ravish his friend's mouth with a kiss. From there, the two of them tugged and grabbed at each other's clothes and whatever bits of skin they managed to reveal until they were in serious danger of losing themselves completely.

"We cannot do this here," Red panted, pushing himself away from Luc suddenly and rocking to his feet. He brushed himself off, regretting the visibility of the bulge in his breeches, and glanced around to make certain no one was in the vicinity who might have seen them. "I think it's time we return to the Abbey."

"I quite agree," Luc said in a deliciously hoarse voice.

The two of them tidied up their picnic, throwing the remnants into the hamper, then straightened themselves up as much as possible before heading home. The school and the cave would have to wait for another day. If not for the meal they'd just hastily eaten, Red would have broken into a run to make it to the safety of his brother's estate as quickly as possible. He wanted Luc as desperately as ever. Their rapport was back to exactly what it was supposed to be. If they could make it home and retire to one of their rooms for the rest of the afternoon—or to the concealed terrace by the lake, providing Anthony and Barrett or Septimus and Adam weren't already there, or even

Percy and his latest conquest, for that matter—Red felt as though he might actually be able to banish his demons enough to breathe.

He should not have been at all surprised, given his luck of late, to discover that Anthony had company, once they made it back to the house. As Red and Luc stumbled through the front door and glimpsed into the afternoon parlor, Red spotted Mr. Haight, the industrialist, taking tea with Anthony and Barrett. Worse still, Anthony caught him coming in.

"Ah, Redmond, there you are," he said in the sort of tone that demanded Red forego whatever plans he had to join them.

With a regretful look to Luc, Red tugged at his jacket to straighten it and entered the parlor. To his surprise, Luc handed the hamper off to Worthington —who had greeted them at the door—and joined him.

"Mr. Haight," Red greeted the newcomer with the sort of joviality that was expected of him once he was in the parlor. He quickly saw that Percy, Septimus, and Clarence were all taking tea with the man as well. "What a pleasure to see you again."

"And you, Lord Beverly," Haight greeted him with a grandfatherly smile. "I was hoping you would return from your walk," he went on. "Your brother has kindly invited me to stay at Wodehouse Abbey for a bit."

"The Abbey can provide far better accommodations than any inn in town," Anthony rushed to qualify, suspiciously on his guard for some reason. "This way, we will be able to ask more questions about the advances of industry and the building of factories."

Something was off. Red sensed it immediately. The others all smiled and sipped their tea like grand ladies, but there was a sheen of uncertainty in the room that Red couldn't put a finger on. Perhaps discussions about breaking up the estate and selling part of it had become heated before he'd arrived.

"I am surprised to see everyone inside on such a fine day," Red said, studying each of his friends in turn to gauge if their expressions held any clues as to what he'd interrupted. "We've been deeply involved in inventing new games of late that I am certain will revolutionize the sporting world of England."

Haight chuckled. "Yes, I believe that is what I interrupted upon my arrival with Mr. Goddard the other day."

"Lord Beverley and Lord Copeland have invented more than a few excessively diverting games," Percy added with a wink for Red that nearly made Red laugh. "I am certain they would be delighted to teach you to play."

"I would enjoy that," Haight laughed. "Though I fear I am too old for games."

"One is never too old for diversions of any sort," Red said, wondering if he might end up liking the industrialist after all, in spite of his connections to Goddard and his intentions to cannibalize Wodehouse Abbey. "If my brother has invited you to join our raucous company for a time, then I am certain we will have a chance to teach you the rules."

"I feel a bit awkward about imposing on His Grace," Haight admitted. "I wouldn't have dreamed of it, but as it happens, I have a small bit of a connection to your former ship, the *Majesty*."

Red felt as though he'd been punched in the gut. The awkward mood in the room was suddenly explained. His brother and his friends knew full well that the *Majesty* was the very last thing he wanted to think about. And Haight had a connection to the ship?

Perhaps Red had no desire to know the man after all. In fact, the bastard had interrupted what could have been a delightful afternoon of him and Luc tupping until they couldn't see straight.

"Why wait to learn the rules of our newly-invented sports?" he said, his voice pitched a bit too high and with too much of an edge to it. "The afternoon is perfect for sport. None of you should be sitting indoors, like statues in a gallery. Come along." He turned and headed for the door, shoving Luc ahead of him as he went and gesturing for the others to come as well. "Do not sit there growing roots, come out and play."

Any sort of game would be a relief if it meant he could forget anyone had so much as mentioned the *Majesty* or the sea.

6

As Luc watched Red stride out of the parlor, gesturing for everyone else to accompany him, his stomach tied itself in knots. Everything from the timbre of Red's voice to the stiffness in his back as he walked was a clear indication that all was not well with him. There was no question in Luc's mind that Mr. Haight and the mention of the *Majesty* had set him off.

Luc sent a quick look of concern to Barrett before jumping after Red. Even though their eyes only met briefly, Luc could see that Barrett was deeply worried about their friend as well. Malton too. In fact, every man left in the parlor as Red stormed out wore a look that indicated some level of anxiety over Red's behavior, even Mr. Haight.

"I suggest we humor him," Luc heard Malton tell the others as he turned the corner and jogged down the hall to catch Red.

"Are you certain this is advisable?" Luc asked as he fell into step with Red. "Perhaps a moment to sit still with a cup of tea is a better balm to whatever ails you."

Red didn't answer right away, and Luc had to step

behind him again as they passed through a doorway halfway down the portrait gallery that took them outside. Once Luc marched by Red's side again as they headed toward the chest of sporting equipment, Red said, "Yes, games and diversions are always advisable." He ignored Luc's suggestion of tea and calm entirely.

As they crossed the lawn, Red put on a smile that Luc wagered was intended to appear casual and playful, but instead gave him an air of desperation. He threw open the lid of the sporting chest with a little too much conviction once they reached it and began pulling out mallets and balls and even a tennis racquet and tossing them aside indiscriminately.

"It pains me to see you like this, Redmond," Luc spoke softly, resting a hand on Red's shoulder.

Red threw him off sharply, but kept his false smile in place. "See me like what?" he asked without looking Luc in the eyes. "I merely wish to play a game, to show the others some of the ingenious diversions Barrett and I have devised in the last several weeks."

Luc kept his lips pressed firmly together. Diversions were not what Red needed in the moment, but it was all too obvious that his lover would not seek out what he truly needed to put his soul to rest at last.

"Alright," Luc said, thumping Red's shoulder with a rougher, more masculine gesture, though the point was still to touch him and give him reassurance. "We'll show your brother's guest, Mr. Haight, how to play your game."

Red straightened abruptly and narrowed his eyes at Luc, as though Luc had misspoken. His brittle expression softened a moment later as whatever Red saw in Luc's eyes calmed him. Red thrust a pall-mall mallet into Luc's hands. "Any game where I am allowed to smash a ball with a mallet is a good game, as far as I am concerned." He turned to the others—who had been approaching slowly, but with an air of caution, as though they did not wish to interrupt the conversation—and went on. "Everyone take a mallet and a ball. This first game is a simple one. It is a contest to see who can hit their ball across the lawn and back the fastest."

Luc stepped away, selecting a ball and lining up on the grass. Perhaps physical exertion would calm Red after all. Smacking a pall-mall ball with full strength did feel good when one needed to vent frustrations. Luc only wished he was convinced it would help when he glanced back to Red. Tension radiated from the man like an unpleasant odor.

Barrett, Septimus, Clarence, Spencer, Malton, and even Lord Sigglesthorpe all came forward to fetch a mallet and ball from the chest, but Mr. Haight hung back. "I'm afraid I am far too advanced in years to race about the lawn in such a way," he said with a jovial laugh.

Luc rather liked the man, in spite of his dubious intent as an industrialist, but Red glared at him.

"You will play the game, sir, or you will cease to call yourself a man," he insisted.

Luc's heart dropped warily to his gut. "If he does not wish to play, Red," he murmured, stepping closer to Red, "you should not force him. He is your brother's guest." He added in a whisper.

The others looked equally upset by Red's rudeness. All but Mr. Haight himself.

"I suppose I could give it a try," the man said, continuing to smile indulgently at Red. "If there are any mallets left. You've quite a few players already."

"We've combined more than one pall-mall set,"

Red said, reaching into the box and pulling out another mallet and ball. "There's plenty for everyone to play."

It was the oddest game Luc had ever taken part in. Red was twice as enthusiastic about his invented sport than he'd been with any of the other made-up games they'd played for the past few days. Everyone else was deeply wary of Red's behavior and eyed him as though he were a tiger that might escape his cage at any moment. Oddly enough, Mr. Haight remained calm throughout the whole thing, even though it was clear to Luc that his age and overall physical condition was not nearly what it should have been for a sport as wild as Red was wont to create.

Luc considered it his duty to his host and to his lover to keep up with Red's vigor, even if the others held back.

"Do you call that an effective blow?" he teased Red as the two of them smashed their balls to the far side of the lawn ahead of the others, running after them so that they could strike again. He felt the need to move heaven and earth to keep Red's spirits up, even if it was at his own expense.

"You should tell me," Red laughed, the sound genuine, though it still had an edge to it. "You are the expert on the subject of blowing."

The ribald quip was almost enough to convince Luc that whatever demon was chasing Red had left him alone, but a moment later, Red smashed his pallmall ball with enough force, his face contorting into a mask of pain and frustration, that Luc knew it was only a temporary reprieve.

"A wager, then?" he panted, dashing to keep up with Red as they reached the designated point to turn around and head back across the lawn. "Loser instructs the winner in the art of blowing by example?"

Red laughed aloud, his shoulders loosening slightly, as he turned to clobber his pall-mall ball, sending it back across the lawn. "I'll take that wager."

A hint of relief filled Luc. He would drop to his knees and swallow Red until he choked, with or without the others looking on, if he thought it would relax the man enough to coax him into a conversation about the dragon of Shaw's death sitting on his shoulder. He was at an utter loss to determine what else might help.

That relief was woefully short-lived as his and Red's progress in the game took them back through the ranks of the others, who were still traveling toward the far end of the lawn.

"Have a care," Red called out with false jollity, then smashed his shoulder into Spencer as they passed each other.

Spencer—who likely hadn't heard Red as he concentrated on hitting his ball—was taken by surprise and thrown back. He sprawled to the ground with a grunt, his mallet flying out of his hand.

"Redmond!" Malton shouted at him, no longer even trying to feign interest in the game.

"It's all in fun, Tony," Red called over his shoulder to his brother, then dashed on.

"He isn't usually this much of a disgrace," Luc caught Barrett telling Malton as the two of them gave up playing the game entirely. "In fact, I've never seen him so agitated before."

"I know what the matter is," Luc panted quietly to them as he ran past, more eager to keep up with Red than ever.

Red was clearly going to win the game, not that

there would be much victory in it. He seemed to know as well, but when he crossed paths with Mr. Haight— who was well behind the others, puffing a bit as he jogged behind his ball, but smiling all the same—Red paused.

"Put some effort into it, old man," Red shouted, his face pinched with frustration. "You are an embarrassment to your name if you continue to play this way."

At last, Mr. Haight's cheerful smile dropped. "I beg your pardon, young man?" he balked.

"Do you have anchors in your breeches or balls, like a man should have? Run, man! Play the game!" Red continued to shout.

"Redmond, stop this at once," Luc hissed as he caught up with Red. "Can you not see that Mr. Haight is winded?"

Evidently, all Red could see was that he was in danger of losing the silly game to Luc. He shot into motion once more, smacking his ball hard and turning the final moments of the game into a race.

In the end, Red won, but he didn't seem to take any pleasure in his victory—as well he shouldn't, as far as Luc was concerned. Luc loved him, but Red's behavior was abominable. Red didn't even speak to Luc once he crossed the finish line. He gave his ball one final smack, then walked off in a circle, panting and wiping the sweat from his brow. He didn't stop walking once his circle was finished. He continued pacing, his shoulders rising and falling tightly, as though he might burst into sobs at any moment.

It was agony for Luc to see the man he loved so painfully distressed, but unless Red chose to speak of the things that haunted him, Luc didn't know what he could do to help. He'd seen men who had been affected by the war grapple with their pain in

Portsmouth, but Red's distress went far beyond any of that.

"Has he been like this since his arrival?" he asked Malton once the game was over and the two of them stood off to the side on their own, taking a moment to catch their breaths. Red already had his head in the sporting chest, sorting through its contents as though he would create another game, which only added to Luc's concern.

Barrett, who stood by Malton's side, shook his head. "He seemed perfectly well when we first arrived. Perhaps he experienced a bit of strain during the impromptu house party we were forced to host a fortnight ago. The house was inundated with strangers."

Luc's brow shot up. He'd only heard mention of the house party and not the full story behind it.

"Red always has been the jolly one in the family," Malton said in a low growl, rubbing his chin as he studied Red at the sporting chest. "There is a distinct difference in his behavior now, though. Perhaps I simply didn't notice it at first. I am accustomed to him being jolly, but this behavior is manic."

"It's Shaw," Luc sighed, scrubbing his face to both clear away the sweat and to release his frustration. "It can only be Shaw. The boy's death has deeply affected him, but he will not speak of the matter."

"Shaw?" Malton glanced between Luc and Barrett in confusion.

"The midshipman," Barrett told him, arching one eyebrow.

Malton made a sound as though he suddenly understood. So Barrett had informed him of the matter after all. None of them seemed to have a solution for the conundrum, though.

"Come on, man!" Red's sudden, frustrated shout

drew them out of their conversation. "Are you a man or a mouse? Run, you bastard, run!"

Dread hit Luc's stomach as he followed the line of Red's sight to find that he was shouting at Mr. Haight again. Poor Mr. Haight looked to be doing his best to finish the game as Clarence and Lord Sigglesthorpe walked on either side of him, encouraging him. That did not in any way excuse Red's behavior, though.

Luc hissed a curse under his breath and marched over to Red. "Enough of this," he said, grasping Red's arm and yanking him away. He pulled Red up the lawn toward the house. "You are behaving like a child, Redmond. If Captain Wallace were here, he would have you keelhauled."

"Let go of me." Red shook out of Luc's grip. He continued to walk with Luc up to the house, and once they were inside the portrait gallery, he spat, "I despise that man and everything he stands for."

"Mr. Haight?" Luc's brow shot up in surprise at the vehemence of Red's statement.

"He is a pirate come to pillage Wodehouse Abbey," Red insisted, beginning to pace along the gallery.

"He is an old man and a factory owner who wishes to discuss business matters with your brother," Luc said, fighting to keep his voice measured when he would rather have slapped sense into Red. It would have been reprehensible to strike a man who was clearly suffering. "You do not know the man."

"I know enough about him to know that he is a wolf in the sheepfold," Red growled, sending a spiteful look toward the windows of the gallery and the sloping lawn beyond.

"Redmond, listen to yourself." Luc stepped in front of Red, stopping the progress of his pacing and grabbing his shoulders. "This is not like you. You are not a petty man of prejudices. Both of us know the true source of your upset."

Red bristled with raw, painful energy, looking everywhere but at Luc's eyes.

"You are biased against the man because he mentioned the *Majesty*," Luc went on. He grasped the side of Red's face with one hand and forced him to meet his eyes. The pain that Luc saw there was heart-wrenching. "Shaw's death was not your fault. You must stop flogging yourself for it at once."

"It *was* my fault," Red said in a rush of breath and emotion. He sucked in a new, ragged breath a moment later and shook Luc off, standing straighter. "Not a soul on this earth will ever be able to convince me that it was not my fault. But what is done is done. I can no more resurrect Shaw, or any of the other brave men who served and died and will never come home, than I can hold back the tide." He rolled his shoulders, breathed deeply, then put on a smile. "Truly, Luc, you are making this into more than it is. We served in a war. Men die in wars. Do you feel guilt for any of the Frenchmen or Americans we sent to a watery grave?"

Luc clenched his jaw at Red's latest diversionary tactic, particularly as those words only deepened the anxiety and desperation in Red's eyes. "You know it is not the same," he said.

"It is the same in that there is not a damned thing I can do to reverse it," Red argued, the sharpness returning to his words. "Not a damned thing. A young man is dead. His life and dreams wasted. All because I did not—" His words turned into a sudden, painful sob.

"Red, darling," Luc sighed, stepping into Red and pulling him into his arms.

He rested one hand on the side of Red's hot face,

then leaned in to kiss him. It was a tender kiss, meant to soothe and calm, not to ignite the fire of lust within either of them. The lust was there regardless, and always was, no matter what Luc's intentions when he kissed Red. He loved Red far too much not to want him whenever they were near each other, but kissing away the pain and self-loathing that he could feel pouring out of ever inch of Red made the unions of their mouths something more than base satisfaction.

"Yes," Red breathed against Luc's mouth, clasping his arms around Luc's back. "Yes, this is what I need. This makes everything better."

Twin bursts of joy and frustration shot through Luc. He thrilled to the knowledge that Red wanted him, but the rising ardor of Red's kiss made it clear he was wanted for all the wrong reasons.

"There is an unused parlor right over there," Red panted between kisses, fumbling with the buttons of Luc's jacket as he drew him down the gallery. "There is a lock on the door, so no one will disturb us. And I won the game, which means you have forfeited a swallow."

Helpless need flooded Luc as he allowed Red to lead him on into the parlor. Not the need for sexual satisfaction, but the need to make the man he loved feel better. It hurt far too much to see Red torturing himself pointlessly, and even though he knew that the way the two of them tore at each other's clothes and thrust their tongues into each other's mouths as they stumbled into the parlor and locked the door behind them was like poking a finger into a gaping leak in a ship's hull, he couldn't stop himself.

"Anything for you, Red," he gasped, undoing the fall of Red's breeches and scooping his lover's thick cock out. "Anything to make you feel better."

"This always makes me feel much better," Red purred, kissing Luc a few more times before nudging his shoulders so that he sank to his knees. "Nothing feels better than your mouth on—"

His cheeky comment ended with a long moan as Luc closed his mouth over the head of Red's cock, licking the drop of moisture that had already formed there. Luc loved Red's taste, loved the way his erection felt in his mouth. He considered the way he drew Red farther back toward his throat, to the point where his eyes watered, as an act of pure devotion. It was a devotion that aroused him to no end and had him throbbing hard in his breeches, but it was a devotion all the same.

And it was wrong. Deep within him, he knew that the way he moved on Red, using his tongue to stimulate him and his hands at the base of Red's cock to increase the pleasure, was the worst possible thing he could do to alleviate the true suffering his beloved was experiencing. It didn't matter that a jolt of pleasure shot through him as Red grasped tight handfuls of his hair and pulled hard as he made the most obscene noises, or that Luc's blood pumped hard with arousal as Red jerked into his mouth, rushing swiftly toward his climax. Nothing good could come of Luc allowing himself to be used as an instrument for Red to bury his turmoil, but that didn't stop him from groaning and swallowing reflexively as Red came down his throat.

"Lovely. Perfect," Red gasped as he sagged against the wall behind them. He tugged on Luc's jacket to prompt him to stand.

Luc only had time to wipe the saliva and Red's seed briefly on his sleeve before Red pulled him in for a kiss. Red's eagerness and fire blasted all good sense out of Luc's mind, and when Red reached into Luc's unfastened breeches to stroke his cock vigorously, Luc knew he didn't stand a chance of convincing Red to see reason and deal with his pain in a more productive way.

"I've missed you terribly," Red panted between kisses, stroking Luc's prick with the clear intention of bringing him off as swiftly as possible. "You've no idea how badly I've needed this."

"Come to my bed tonight," Luc managed to grind out through the impossible arousal that had him near the point of insensibility. "Or let me come to yours. We should be together, sharing everything. A bed—"

"No," Red gasped just as warm jets of Luc's seed spilled over his hand.

Luc groaned and gasped as Red milked him dry, then sagged into him, his head hitting the wall behind Red's shoulder. They stayed there for a moment, Red still cradling Luc's flagging cock and balls, as they caught their breath. It took a few moments for Luc to realize what Red had said.

"No?" he asked, leaning away and staring hard into Red's eyes. He started tucking himself back into his breeches.

For a few, desperate heartbeats, Luc saw an even greater fear in Red's eyes.

Red shrugged. "We've no need to share a bed," he said. "We never have before."

"This is not before," Luc told him seriously. The man could not be so oblivious that he didn't know the true intent of Luc's suggestion.

But that was precisely the trouble. Red knew what he wanted from him.

Red pushed Luc away and began to tidy up. "As long as there are secluded parlors and clandestine pleasure gardens at Wodehouse Abbey, the two of us have no need to resort to anything as domestic as sharing a bedroom," Red scoffed playfully. "It is not as though the two of us are in love or anything half as silly as that."

Luc's heart stung as though Red had stabbed him. The feeling was made worse by the fact that Red failed to look him in the eyes, to look in his direction at all. Which meant Red was lying to himself. Luc couldn't decide which was worse—Red genuinely thinking their connection was nothing but sexual or knowing the man loved him but was running from that love. And he was wise enough to know that it all boiled down to the same thing.

"Shaw's death was not your fault," he said for what felt like the thousandth time, clipping his words. "It pains me to see you persisting in this belief that it was. Any pain you experience hurts me, Red. It hurts me because I—"

"Please do not ruin what we have, Luc," Red said, barely above a whisper, glancing balefully in Luc's direction. "It is the only thing keeping me from madness."

Luc's mouth dropped open and his entire torso squeezed with unrequited emotion. Red's words were perhaps the cruelest thing that had ever been said to him. He could not bear to stop loving Red or to cease demonstrating that love, but Red would not allow him to express it in any but the basest of ways either. Luc was so stunned and hurt that he couldn't even tell Red off for his cruelty.

In a way, he had no need to. The shame in Red's eyes was enough to tell Luc that the bastard knew. He knew, but he did not have the first idea what to do about it.

The look and emotion they shared dissolved as Red turned away and shook his head. He made the barest hint of a desperate, hopeless sound before striding past Luc, unlocking the door, and marching back into the portrait gallery, leaving Luc feeling as alone and destitute as he'd ever felt.

7

E verything was going wrong, and there was nothing Red could do to stop it. He should have known that he would never be able to hide anything from Luc. The two of them had known each other too well and for too long for Luc to miss the turmoil in Red's soul. It was bad enough that his friend could see just how deeply Shaw's death had affected him, now he had to contend with the one thing that he had tried to ignore, dodge, and make light of for years—Luc's feelings for him.

He was up half the night, tossing and turning and wondering if he would have been as agitated if he'd accepted Luc's invitation to share a bed. The suggestion had nearly stopped his heart when Luc had made it in the parlor after their tryst. There had been a few times in the past—when the crews of the *Majesty* and the *Hawk* had been together on shore leave—when he and Luc had shared a bed all through the night. Red had adored waking with Luc's naked form splayed by his side, their limbs entangled. It felt right and natural for them to slumber together and to awaken in each other's arms with the dawn light.

But everything had changed since then. Red's

nightmares alone were reason to keep Luc as far away from his bed as possible. Beyond that, the implication of the two of them sharing something so domestic now that their lives in the Navy were over was more than Red could bear. He wanted it the way he wanted air in his lungs and sunshine on his face, but he did not deserve something so wonderful.

He did not deserve Luc's love, and Luc was most definitely in love with him.

Paradoxically, that sure and certain knowledge filled Red with misery and pushed him into a foul mood as he washed and dressed after a mostly sleepless night. He was certain that he had disgraced himself in front of his brother and his friends so much the day before that they would treat him like the enemy when he went down for breakfast.

In fact, they were wary as soon as he entered the room, but the looks they sent him as he silently moved to the sideboard to pile a plate with ham and eggs were more concerned than venomous. Which was ten times worse.

"And as soon as construction can begin on those few, small fixes," Septimus was telling Spencer in a loud voice as Red made his way to the table and sat sullenly, "we should be able to start taking applications for teachers."

"Good, good," Spencer said with a nod. "At least one of us has found a life after the war."

"Barrett has found a life as well, haven't you, Barry," Clarence teased Barrett with a wink. "Life as a duchess suits you."

The others laughed. Red couldn't even manage a smile. He ate his breakfast with a sinking feeling. The meal was notable more for who was not present than who was. Luc hadn't come down yet. In spite of the vehemence of Red's internal insistence that he didn't care for Luc that way, his absence felt like a chair missing at the table. The room was without color as long as Luc wasn't in it.

Percy wasn't there either. Red distracted himself from thoughts of Luc by speculating which of the footmen had warmed Percy's bed the night before and whether Anthony would sack the lad if he found out. Adam was missing as well, but Red figured that had something to do with the ague that both Eliza and Francis had caught a few days before—an illness that had confined them to the nursery. Ivy would see to their care, but knowing Adam, he would stay with the children as well.

The most notable absence, however, was Haight's.

"Has your industrialist decided to relocate to Hull after all?" Red asked Anthony once the conversation reached a lull. "Has he been insulted enough for one visit?" He wasn't certain if his words sounded bitter and sullen or if they'd come out contrite. He wasn't even certain how he'd meant them to be heard.

Anthony stared hard at him for a long while before saying, "Mr. Haight was exhausted after the events of yesterday and asked to take breakfast in his room this morning, but he is still in residence with us."

Red might not have known how he felt about his own feelings, but Anthony was most definitely put out with him. He had to admit that his brother had reason to be vexed. All he could do in response was nod and pour himself another cup of tea.

"Where is Luc this morning?" he asked without meeting any of his friends' eyes.

A short silence followed before Barrett said, "We assumed he was with you."

Red glanced up to find everyone at the table watching him with particular interest. "No," he said definitively. "Luc is very much *not* with me." He intended his words to be a broader statement than merely information about where Luc had not spent the night.

In response, the others glanced amongst themselves, sending doubtful and worried looks across the table. It made Red feel as though they all thought he should be committed to Bedlam, but they had yet to work out how to bring the matter up with him.

"I was thinking that I might write to George and ask to visit him, Maria, and the children for a time," he told Anthony. The notion of escaping to George's house had only just hit him, but it sounded like a very good idea indeed.

It was an idea that made everyone else at the table stop what they were doing to gape at him once more. And it helped nothing that Luc chose exactly that moment to walk into the breakfast room.

"What is this?" Luc asked, his expression stricken. "You have plans to leave?"

"It is a fresh idea," Red said, guilt stabbing at him as he sawed through his piece of ham. "I have yet to make any decisions on the matter."

"I would hope," Luc began, his voice emotional and unregulated, but then stopped. He cleared his throat as he walked to the sideboard and took up a plate, then tried again in a much more measured tone. "I would hope that, seeing as those of us from the *Hawk* have just arrived, that you would postpone this excursion to spend more time with us."

He was upset. With one comment that he had not thought through, Red had upset the one person who was trying the hardest to bring him comfort. As it happened, Luc was also the one person who disquieted him more than anyone else, but that didn't mean he could hurt his friend without impunity.

"Perhaps it would be best for all," he said, focused on his plate when Luc took the seat beside him. "I fear that Wodehouse Abbey might not be the best place for me at the moment."

"The best place for you is with your friends and your family," Luc argued in his soft voice. That voice was like a rapier wrapped in silk, and it gutted Red every time.

"George and his family are my family as well," he snapped in reply. "And I have yet to offend or unsettle him and any guests he might have."

"You have not offended or unsettled us, Red," Barrett tried to argue with him.

"No?" Red glanced across the table at him. It rankled that Barrett was trying to be kind to him. All of his friends were trying to be kind. He did not want that sort of kindness from the men he had served with in battle, the men who had drunk too much rum with him and in front of whom he had embarrassed himself in numerous ribald ways. He did not want their sympathy when they knew just as well as he did from their time in His Majesty's Navy what constituted a strong and noble officer and what made someone a disgrace unworthy of his rank.

It was too much for him to bear. He threw down his knife and fork and stood.

"If you will excuse me," he said, wiping his mouth with his serviette, then throwing that down as well. "I have no wish to be in such esteemed company at the moment. I think I will go for a walk."

To his surprise, as he strode out of the room, Spencer stood and called out, "I'll come with you."

The offer was enough of a surprise that Red paused in the doorway and waited for Spencer to catch up to him. He steadfastly refused to look at Luc as he did, though he could feel Luc's gaze on him as though it were a caress. It was a relief once he and Spencer continued down the hall and away from the others.

"Forgive me for being shocked at your offer of company," he told Spencer, careful to position himself on the side with Spencer's good ear and to speak loudly enough for the man to hear him. "You and I have never been particularly close friends."

"But I have always considered you a friend," Spencer said, apparently alarmed at Red's categorization of their friendship as they stepped outside into the bright, morning light.

"Yes, of course," Red said, shaking his head and cursing himself for getting something else wrong. "We most certainly are friends."

Spencer smiled and nodded. "I had hoped so. But to be honest, I needed to get away from the others."

"Truly?" Red's brow shot up in surprise.

Spencer's face pinched as they started down the path that would take them into the wood. "I find it difficult and embarrassing to be in a conversation with more than one person speaking at a time. My...my hearing is worse than I have let on, and I find that I can barely navigate the world after...." He let his sentence drop, but Red understood immediately that he was referring to his battle wounds.

"I can understand that," he said, relaxing and falling into a companionable walk with Spencer. "The war has left all of us with scars of one sort or another."

Part of Red had hoped that he'd spoken too quietly for Spencer to hear, but Spencer glanced at him with a strained look. "Nobody blames you, Redmond."

The fact that he failed to specify what people could blame him for was as bad as if Spencer had railed at him for his negligence.

"I blame myself," he said, deliberately too quiet for Spencer to hear.

Spencer made a sound and shook his head, but didn't comment. The two of them walked on, down the slope and into the dappled sun and shade of the wood. Red had hoped walking with Spencer would make him feel better, but it only tightened the band of anxiety around his chest. Spencer was a good man, a serious man. He was a better man than Red. So why had Spencer been the one to lose most of his hearing after the cannon blast and not him? Where was the justice in that?

"I have enjoyed this wood more than any other part of your family's estate," Spencer said once the silence between them had extended for too long and Red's guilt-riddled contemplation of justice had him bristling. "I find it quaint and ideal for contemplation. Your brother mentioned that it was planted deliberately by an ancestor?"

"Yes, by my great-grandfather," Red said, though his heart was still too restless to truly enjoy sharing that bit of family history. "He was enamored of the legend of Robin Hood, but forests like Sherwood do not grow in Yorkshire. So he imported hundreds of trees and had the wood planted. It isn't much by some standards, but it is enough to make for an interesting feature, and to provide a home for various species of deer and other small animals."

Spencer hummed. Red's shoulders unbunched. Perhaps the wood was a good idea after all, if it meant one could escape from the rest of the estate and the world for a time. Spencer had the right way of things by visiting it.

Or so Red thought until they were startled by the screech of a hawk and the flutter of its wings as it swooped near them.

"Hermes, no!" A moment later, young Declan Shelton, the estate's gamekeeper, dashed out of the trees and onto the path. Declan stopped abruptly with a sharp intake of breath, his eyes going wide at the sight of Red and Spencer.

Declan wasn't the only one who gasped. Red had encountered the handsome and reclusive young gamekeeper a handful of times since returning home, but in that moment of surprise, he was struck by how small and innocent Declan appeared. More precisely, Red was struck by how closely Declan resembled the midshipmen on the various ships he'd sailed on or visited.

Red saw Shaw in Declan's eyes. It was unavoidable. The two did not resemble each other, but the similarity was there all the same. It hurt more than Red could have anticipated, particularly since he wasn't ready for the sight.

"Forgive me," he said, his voice hoarse and his nerves frayed. "I must go."

"Redmond?" Spencer called after him.

Red ignored Spencer's concern and marched back the way they'd come. As soon as he'd traveled along enough of the twists and turns of the path to be out of sight of Spencer and Declan, Red broke into a run.

He didn't stop running until he was out of the cool shade of the wood and bathed in the bright sunlight of the yard. Sunlight of the sort that had shone down that morning when Shaw fell to his death. It was devilishly unfair, all of it. A boy like Shaw should have had a whole life ahead of him. He shouldn't have died because Red had been too much of a coward to tell the boys to stop playing in the rigging. It was unfair that he couldn't run far enough or fast enough to banish the sound of that sickening thump from his mind, or the shouts and tears that had followed.

He avoided the house, running around the edge of the wood toward the wilder fields of Wodehouse Abbey, where few people ever ventured. He needed to get as far away from everything as he possibly could so that he could forget. He needed to—

"Oh! Good heavens!"

His thoughts and his steps stopped abruptly when he came around the far edge of the woods and spotted Haight standing in the middle of the tall grass. The breeze coming from the ocean a mile away had the grass swaying like water, and dotted with wildflowers as it was, the whole thing was fragrant and lovely. It was completely incongruous to find Haight standing there like another weed.

"Mr. Haight?" Red asked, panting from his impromptu run.

Of all things, Haight turned bright pink and looked flustered and embarrassed. "I can explain," he said quickly, his jaw flapping and his eyes wide. "It was just a little walk. To survey the land of the estate, you see. I have seen so little of it, and...." The man's words tapered off as he studied Red. He must have come to the conclusion that Red was as sheepish at being caught in Haight's presence as Haight was to be found wandering alone on a deserted corner of the estate.

Red had ruined enough things already in the last few days. An opportunity to set something right, for a change, stood right in front of him, and he was obligated to take it.

"Mr. Haight, I must apologize for my unforgivable behavior yesterday," he said, closing the gap between them slowly, as though Haight would realize he had every reason to be angry with Red and would rail at him. "I was upset for other reasons, you see, and I foolishly vented those emotions where I should not have."

To Red's surprise, Haight's expression melted into a fatherly smile. "I have committed indiscretions like that myself more times than I can count, young man." He added a pleasant laugh for good measure. "Young men, like yourself, are still slaves to the whims and sentiments of youth. If it is forgiveness you are searching for, I forgive you."

The words came so unexpectedly and struck so deep that Red's eyes stung with surprise tears. Forgiveness. It was something he hadn't even dared to contemplate. His soul instantly longed for it, but only for the briefest moment. He frowned and blinked his tears away, clearing his throat and moving to stand by Haight's side. Together, they surveyed the field.

"I take it you are assessing the land you wish to purchase for your wicked factory?" Red asked. He had no desire whatsoever to discuss himself and his concerns any more than he already had, and the best way to turn a conversation was to have someone talk about themselves.

"You have found me out," Haight admitted with a pleasantly ashamed look. "Your family owns quite an extensive bit of prime land here in Yorkshire. The access to the coast alone is reason to consider it for a factory."

Red frowned. "Do you truly believe that it is right

to cover over all this pristine countryside with an abomination that belches smoke and soot and crushes the livelihoods of small craftsmen?"

Haight surprised him once again by spreading his hands and sending Red an almost apologetic look. "Once the wheel of progress has begun to turn, it is impossible to stop. Not a soul in England, in the world, can observe the changes that have taken place in the last few decades, in mining and in manufacturing, or note the fortunes those changes have brought without concluding that the way forward is absolute and irreversible. Is it better to expend one's energy holding back the tide, as you naval men might say, or is it better to seek out ways to meet the changes with intelligence and an eye to better the lives of everyone involved?"

Red felt as though Haight's explanation had taken the wind out of him. "Do you truly believe the changes of which you speak will brighten the futures of the poor souls who seek employment in your factories in the coming years?"

He thought of Shaw, of the young man's dreams to travel the world, to see so many things. Would Shaw have ended up as a worker shackled to a spinning machine or a water frame, or some new contraption that had yet to be thought of? If he had, would he have craved death instead?

Red shook his head as he and Haight walked slowly across the field in the direction of the house. "Is it right for so few men to control the profit of production and the wellbeing of those young people who will leave the safety of their homes for the perils of a life at sea." Only when he finished speaking did he realize he'd said something other than what he'd intended to say. "That is, the perils of working in the midst of large and dangerous machinery. That is what I meant." He frowned at himself in confusion.

Haight paused and fixed Red with a curious look. "You speak as though you are not a member of the aristocracy, my lord," he said. "Have your sort not controlled a vast amount of the wealth of England for centuries?"

Red's face burned and his back itched with uncertainty. He attempted to tell himself it was because of the sun beating down on him and the sweat from his anxious run drying under his clothes. "I have seen young lives cut short unjustly," he said, each word bitter on his tongue.

Haight let out a breath and rested a hand on Red's arm as though he were Red's father. "I know," he said simply.

The hair on the back of Red's neck stood up, and for a moment, Red was struck with the alarming notion that Haight did, indeed, know. He knew precisely what had Red mired in turmoil. The prospect terrified him until Haight went on with, "I have overseen spinning and weaving mills for over a decade now. I have seen horrific injuries and accidents that could have been prevented. I have not been insensible to these things, not at all. My deepest desire is to assist with the advancement of industry while also searching for ways to minimize injury and illness as a result of mankind's constant greed. But sometimes accidents happen. When you come to be my age, my lord, you will see that. It does not mean we should abandon our endeavors altogether."

Another chill shot down Red's spine. There was too much compassion in Haight's eyes. The man spoke too much sense as well. And he smiled at Red as though they both understood a secret that few others had ever encountered.

Dammit, but Red liked the old man. In spite of what he had come to Wodehouse Abbey to do, and in spite of the almost preternatural way he seemed to reach into Red's heart and soul without knowing the first thing about what troubled him.

If only Haight could solve the problem of how to stop a dear, good man from loving him. For Luc's own sake, their affair could not sink beneath their skins and into their hearts.

"Tell me more about what sort of factory you have in mind for Wodehouse Abbey," he said as they strode on. With any luck, learning about all of the advancements Haight spoke of would not only distract him from his troubles, it would distract him from the even greater problem he had created for himself and his heart by indulging in what he'd hoped would ease his mind. Something told him that not even the spinning of the world into a new era could divert Red's full focus from Luc, though.

8

Luc's chest ached pitifully when Red stormed out of the breakfast room. Irrational though it was, he couldn't help but feel as though he'd failed Red in some way. All he wanted was to be a balm to Red's troubled soul, but instead, he feared he'd made things worse. At least Spencer accompanied him on whatever restless walk Red felt he needed to take.

With a sigh that he did his best to suppress, Luc pried his eyes away from the breakfast room doorway, only to find that the others at the table were watching him.

"He cannot continue to be an arse forever," Clarence reassured him with the closest thing to a gentle look that Clarence was capable of.

"You have not known my brother long, have you?" Malton mumbled in return, frowning at the empty doorway. He turned his gaze to Luc. "I feel as though I must apologize for my brother's behavior," he said. "And I must apologize for failing to see the signs of his distress earlier."

Luc shook his head and cut into his ham one last time before deciding he didn't have the appetite for the rest of his breakfast. He set his knife and fork down and leaned back in his chair. "I am not certain that any of us read the signs of Red's distress accurately," he said. "As you most likely know, Red is quite adept at masking his true feelings behind joviality and fun."

Barrett snorted and shook his head, stabbing a bit of egg on his plate particularly fiercely. "I love the man like a brother, but he vexes me to no end."

"I love him as far more than a brother," Luc said quietly, staring at his plate without really seeing it, "and he breaks my heart."

The table went silent again. Luc could feel the sympathy pouring off of the others, but he wasn't certain he was entirely comfortable with it. Sympathy danced with pity more often than not, and he was most certainly not a man to be pitied. He'd been born into a prosperous family of the middle class, he'd always excelled in his studies, and his father had been gracious enough to pay for his commission in the Royal Navy. He'd served honorably, gained distinction for himself, and was thought of highly by his superiors. Now he stood on the precipice of being one of a tiny handful of men offered a captaincy in the post-war Navy. One could argue that he had nothing at all to be gloomy about and that his life promised to be filled with nothing but accomplishment and glory.

But that life would mean nothing to him if it caused him to leave Red behind, particularly when Red was in a state.

"I approve of you, if you had any concerns in that regard." Malton's kind comment caught Luc off-guard and shook him out of his thoughts.

"I beg your pardon, Your Grace?" He blinked at the

man, wondering if the conversation had gone on without him while he'd been away with the fairies.

Malton smiled awkwardly. "I approve of your connection to my brother," he repeated. "Should you be wondering about that."

"I—" Luc had too many other things occupying his mind to give the first thought as to whether the Duke of Malton approved of him. "Thank you, Your Grace."

"Anthony, please," the man said, pushing back his chair and standing. The others seemed to be done with breakfast as well, so Luc stood and abandoned his place. "Would you accompany me upstairs to the nursery to look in on my children? They've been unwell, as you know, and I believe they would enjoy a bit of company."

"The children adore company," Barrett added as the three of them made their way across the hall to the stairs and started up.

Of course, as Luc suspected, Malton—that is, Anthony—had another motive for inviting Luc along to the nursery.

"What is the Admiralty's view of the accident that killed the midshipman?" he asked.

Luc was certain Barrett had told him that no one aboard the *Majesty* believed Red was to blame as well, but Barrett must have also told him that Luc had the strongest connection to the Admiralty still of any of their band of friends.

"They view the incident as a tragic accident as well," he reported with a sigh, rubbing a hand over his face. "Discipline was lax across the entire fleet after the official end of the war, once we all knew we'd be sailing home. Neither the *Majesty* nor the *Hawk* had seen any sort of engagement for weeks, nor did we expect to. I know that Redmond believes his negligence and lack of enforcing the usual rules was something he should be blamed for, but every officer aboard his ship and mine had long since given up keeping a tight rein on their crews."

"So the way he oversaw activity on the deck that day was not unusual?" Anthony asked as they rounded a corner and headed up the last staircase to the floor that contained the nursery.

"Not unusual at all," Luc said. "And the Admiralty knows it. In fact, when they intimated that they would give me another command and I requested Red be considered as my first-mate, they seemed open to the idea."

"Which means the burden of wrongdoing is all in Redmond's head," Anthony sighed as they reached the top of the stairs and headed down the hall.

"I am afraid so." Luc paused, hanging back a bit before they reached the nursery and the conversation would, out of care for the children's sensibilities, cease. "Redmond was fond of Midshipman Shaw," he said. "We all were. He was a bright and energetic lad with a promising future ahead of him. It was tragic that his future was not to be. I think it is the guilt Redmond feels for that, for the fact that he has been gifted with a future when Shaw, and so many others, have not, that truly eats away at his soul."

Anthony nodded and smiled sadly, then clapped a hand on Luc's shoulder to indicate his approval before they all headed on to the nursery proper.

It was poignant to visit with Anthony's children so soon after thinking about Oliver Shaw. Luc had taken to Lady Eliza and Lord Francis as soon as he'd met them on his first day at the Abbey, and even with their noses drippy and their heads troubled with catarrh, they were good company.

"Mr. Seymour showed me how to cut paper figures," Lord Francis informed Luc as they all sat at a small table that was designed for children, his words distorted by congestion. "See? I've made a boat."

A large paper boat had been cut out of some sort of brown paper, and Lord Francis and Lady Eliza had drawn figures for their Uncle Red, Barrett, and each of their new friends.

"This one is you," Lady Eliza pointed out a finely-drawn figure with a wide smile who stood atop the foredeck, sniffling as she did.

"We are learning the names of the parts of a ship today rather than working on mathematics or French grammar," Seymour informed Anthony with a wink.

"A wise decision." Anthony nodded his approval.

Luc thought it was an ingenious lesson, and he joined in, quizzing the sniffling, drippy children on the names of each of the sails and masts. Doing so caused a different sort of pain in his heart as they came to the parts of the foremast, from which Shaw had fallen. Red wasn't the only one who had been affected by the death, it just seemed as though he was the only one failing to come to terms with it. And now he had plans to run away and avoid both his pain and his pleasure entirely.

"Do you think Red truly will go visit your brother, George?" he asked rather suddenly as the children repositioned their paper friends around the ship.

Both children stopped playing and gasped, looking to Anthony.

"Uncle Red isn't going away, is he, Papa?" Lady Eliza asked.

"He cannot go away," Lord Francis agreed. "Is it because we are sick? Is he angry because we are sick?"

"No, dear ones, it is not that at all," Anthony reassured them with a kiss to each of their heads. "It was idle talk at breakfast this morning. I can assure you that Uncle Red is going nowhere." He glanced to Luc as he spoke. "In fact, I will write to Uncle George immediately to inform him of the situation and to kindly refuse his hospitality, should Uncle Red decide to be an arse and go anyhow."

"Papa! You said arse!" Lord Francis gasped.

Anthony chuckled and ruffled the boy's hair. "Do not tell anyone."

Luc chuckled at the domestic moment. It was a relief to know that he had support in his efforts to help Red face his demons, and from as kind a man as Anthony, but he was still at a complete loss as to how he could bring an end to Red's suffering. Particularly since Red seemed to bound and determined to continue to suffer. Luc had yet to uncover a means to resolve the whole thing.

The playtime in the nursery was interrupted a short time later when Worthington appeared in the doorway.

"Your Grace, Mr. Goddard is here," the butler announced with a sour expression. "He wishes to speak to Mr. Haight—who I believe has gone for a morning walk—and to you."

Anthony sighed and grimaced as he pushed himself to stand. Barrett and Luc rose with him. Luc had the feeling Anthony wanted to mutter a string of expletives that would have put even the most hardened sailor to shame, but not with the children present. "I suppose there is no way out of this," he said instead as the three of them started to the door.

Everything Luc had learned about Mr. Goddard so far was unpleasant. He braced himself for an irritating confrontation, even though it would be a confrontation with Anthony. He was taken completely by surprise when his first reaction to the sight of the man was to snort with amusement. Goddard might have come to speak to Anthony, but Lord Sigglesthorpe had found him first.

"Pray tell, what precisely is it that a land broker does?" Sigglesthorpe asked from his seat on the small sofa where Goddard had apparently been placed to wait. Sigglesthorpe was dressed in lavender and green that morning. His breeches were cut obscenely tight, and he had his legs crossed toward Goddard. In fact, he leaned exceedingly close to Goddard, smiling prettily at him.

"I...er...um...." Goddard writhed in his place, sending a sidelong glance to Sigglesthorpe, as though he was at a loss for what to do. Sigglesthorpe was a lord, after all. "We facilitate the sale and transfer of land from one owner's hands to another," he mumbled.

"I do so like hands," Sigglesthorpe said, twisting his entire body toward Goddard and scooting closer. Goddard was already at the edge of the sofa and could go no farther. Sigglesthorpe brushed his fingers across the back of Goddard's hand, then threaded their fingers together. "You have such strong, fine hands, sir."

"Oh...well...do I?" Goddard cleared his throat. He did not immediately pull his hand away from Sigglesthorpe's though, and if Luc hadn't known better—and if Goddard hadn't seen Anthony enter the room—he figured there was a chance Goddard might actually succumb to Sigglesthorpe's charms.

It was Sigglesthorpe who brought the flirtation to an abrupt end by nearly bounding off the sofa to greet the newcomers. "Your Grace, I have made your caller, Mr. Goddard, feel quite welcome this morning."

"Yes, thank you, Percy," Anthony said in a low growl, sending Sigglesthorpe a flat stare of disapproval. He couldn't hide the amusement in his eyes, though. "Mr. Goddard, to what do we owe the pleasure?" he asked.

Luc didn't hear the man's initial response. Sigglesthorpe swayed his way over to him and Barrett, then lowered his voice to say, "I trust you can forgive me for making a spectacle of myself. Under usual circumstances, I would never thrust myself upon a man who clearly has no interest, but I wagered that ninny could use a little discomfiting before inflicting whatever stupidity he has on our host."

Luc and Barrett both burst into sniggers that they had a difficult time hiding. Goddard had risen from the sofa to face Anthony, and both men turned to frown at their giggling trio with varying degrees of annoyance.

"So I will not allow you to undermine any chance I have of earning a commission on the land sale, Your Grace," Goddard said, apparently finishing up whatever thought he'd shared with Anthony to begin with. "Which is why I must speak with Mr. Haight at once."

"I believe my butler has informed you that Mr. Haight is enjoying a morning walk, since it is such a fine day," Anthony told the man losing every trace of amusement. "If you wish, you can await his return here. I will have tea brought up, if you'd like."

"I would," Goddard said with a nod toward Worthington that contained far too much arrogance, as far as Luc was concerned. "And while we wait, I should very much like, Your Grace, for you to tell me whether you intend to proceed with the sale of your land."

Anthony looked as though he'd rather have crocodiles snack on his balls. "I have not decided," he said, glancing to Worthington.

Worthington nodded in return, but before he turned away to see about tea, he caught Luc's eyes and gestured for him to join him in the hall. Curious, Luc followed him.

"Mr. Goddard arrived with the post," Worthington said, striding over to a small table at the side of the room and retrieving a letter. "This arrived for you. I trusted that I should give it to your right away."

"Thank you, Worthington," Luc said with an excited smile, taking the letter.

It was clear at a glance that it was the letter from the Admiralty he'd been waiting for. Heart pounding against his ribs, he tore into it. The stationary bore the official seal of the Admiralty, and as Luc's eyes flew over the page, his smile widened. The letter contained everything he'd been waiting for.

"Good news?" Barrett asked, wandering into the hall.

Before answering him, Luc smirked and asked in return, "Do you not have the stomach for Goddard's conversation?"

Barrett let out a frustrated growl and crossed the hall to Luc. "That man is a nuisance, and the sooner Anthony rids himself of him the better."

"Is he going to sell the land to Haight?" Luc asked.

"I honestly do not know." Barrett shrugged and shook his head, then nodded to the letter in Luc's hands. "What does the Admiralty say?"

"It is as I'd hoped," Luc said, barely able to contain a burst of joyful laughter. "They wish to give me command of *HMS Daphne*. She's a small ship, but she will be deployed to the far east to help protect trade with India and beyond."

"That is wonderful news, Luc." Barrett clapped a hand on his shoulder. "When does she depart?"

"In less than a month," he said, bubbling with excitement. "In fact, the Admiralty requires my presence in Portsmouth in just over a week's time."

"A week?" The words were nearly shouted in desperation by Red as he stood only a few yards away from Luc and Barrett, Haight by his side. The two men must have entered the house through a back door, and had come up the hall as Luc was speaking. They were rosy-cheeked and glowing, as if they'd enjoyed a long walk in the sun. Luc would have taken it as a good sign, were it not for Red's bereft expression.

A tremor of anxiety shot through Luc, but he reminded himself that the turn of events was a good one, and that it could provide a way for him to help Red grow past the tragedy of the *Majesty*. "You may see the letter, if you'd like," he said, stepping away from Barrett and drawing Red into a side parlor with him.

"You would leave the hospitality my brother has offered you so soon after arriving?" Red grew even angrier instead of settling once the two of them were alone.

Luc clenched his jaw for a moment and let out a frustrated breath through his nose. "Were you not, just this morning, speaking of running away to your brother's house? And now you accuse me wrongdoing because the Admiralty has called for me?"

Red snapped away, clenching his jaw and his fists. "It is not the same. George lives within a day's ride of here. India is the other side of the world."

"Precisely," Luc said stepping close enough to Red to rest a hand on his shoulder. "India is far away from everything that has hurt you. And I want you to come with me, as my right hand. I do not wish to go on without you, Red."

Luc thought his words were rather pretty, but instead of melting, as he'd hoped, Red's expression filled with anger and pain.

9

Hearing Luc say not only that he would be leaving within a week, but that he would shortly sail off to the other side of the world, leaving Red completely alone, filled Red with the sensation of falling. It was as if the deck had given way below him and he'd been plunged into a dark abyss, and no matter what he did, he could not save himself.

"I told you, I am never going back to sea," he snapped, turning away from Luc and marching across the room to one of the windows that looked out over the sunshine playing off the lawn.

"I know that you have said that," Luc said in a careful voice, pursuing Red to the other side of the room, "but please consider. You and I would serve on the same ship for a change. We could be together in all of our adventures. As captain, I will have an entire, large cabin to myself, and though it bends the rules, I am certain we could devise a way for us to share that cabin."

"No." Red shook his head violently and stepped away as soon as Luc came close enough to reach for his hand. "You know the Admiralty would never stand for it. Rules are rules."

"And who will enforce those rules when we are out to sea with a carefully-selected crew manning the *Daphne*?" Luc asked.

Red's jaw twitched with tension as he reached the cold fireplace and leaned his arm against the mantel. Luc was only partially right to think shipboard dalliances would go unreported. It was the luck of the draw as to whether all aboard any given ship would keep each other's secrets. One minor officer with a stick up his arse could spell court-martial for clandestine lovers. Love affairs between common seamen could be swept under the carpet and often were, but officers who blatantly broke the law wouldn't have it so easy.

And that was assuming Red wanted to carry on with Luc the way they had been.

As soon as the thought that he didn't actually want Luc so much as whispered to him, the larger portion of his soul roared in protest. He did want Luc. He always had. Bodily, at least. That was the problem.

"I will not return to sea, Lucas." He whipped around to face Luc, unsurprised that Luc had followed him across the room. "I cannot. You know why."

"Yes, I do know why," Luc said, ever patient, but with signs that his patience was wearing thin. His lips pressed in a tight line, and the creases between his brow were furrowing deeper. "Why not think of this voyage as an opportunity to right the wrongs you feel you have committed in the past? You could take charge of the midshipmen on the *Daphne*, teach them everything they need to know, keep them out of harm. You could make up for—"

"I could not," he blurted before Luc had a chance to finish. "It would be too much, and you know it," he conceded as he broke away from the fireplace and marched across the room to a curiosity cabinet filled with ancient, fussy bits of porcelain that one of his female ancestors had once collected. The restlessness he had felt since morning had mounted to the point where he thought he might crawl out of his skin.

"You do not have to decide on this right away." Luc followed him once again. "We have a day or so before I must depart for Portsmouth."

"You would leave me so soon?" he returned to the same argument he'd started with, pain flaring in his gut again.

This time, Luc responded with a terse sigh of frustration. "You were planning to leave me. At least in my scenario, I wish to take you with me." He threw out his arms in a helpless gesture of irritation.

Red's impulse was to remind Luc once again that he barely wanted to look at the sea again, let alone set foot on a ship, but it was clear to him that neither of them would budge from their position and neither would convince the other to see things their way.

"I do not see why it matters to you one way or another what I think of the Navy or the sea," he growled, marching away from the cabinet and back toward the window. God, if he didn't have the opportunity to run or swim or fuck or use his body in some way that would expend the maelstrom of discomfort within him soon, he would run mad. He gazed longingly out to the lawn for a fraction of a second, then jerked back to Luc—who had followed him yet again. "Why should you care if I go with you or not? There is nothing between us besides a bit of fun now and then."

He wanted to take back the words as soon as they were spoken. Luc's face crumpled for the barest heartbeat before contorting into fury. "Is that what you think of me, then?" he hissed, his anger barely controlled. "That I am just some pretty arse to fuck when the urge takes you? Is that all I mean to you?"

"No, Luc, I didn't mean that," Red snapped. He was going mad. He had to be. That was why his skin felt as though it would itch and bristle until he peeled himself out of it.

Luc wasn't appeased at all. "I think that *is* what you mean, only you cannot admit it to yourself. You cannot admit that the only person you care about is yourself." He took a step closer to Red. "You aren't even truly upset about Shaw's death, I'd wager. You are merely grieving the loss of your own good opinion of yourself."

"How dare you say that?" Red gasped, truly hurt.

"How dare you tell me that I am nothing to you?" Luc fired back.

The two of them stood toe to toe, glaring at each other, bristling with emotions that had the air between them crackling. Red was seized by the sudden desire to grasp Luc's face and pull him in for a searing kiss. The urge to throw himself at his friend or bend him over the nearest chair so that he could fuck him raw had him close to growling. But he could not do it. He could not snap the last tenuous string of hope that still bound them together.

"I cannot breathe," he said instead, breaking away from Luc and striding out to the hall so fast it might have been considered a run. "I have to move, to run, to do something or I will go mad," he spoke louder, certain Luc was following him, even though he didn't turn to be certain.

He didn't stop moving until he was outside, and even then, he was too restless to slow his steps. To his surprise, Anthony, Barrett, Haight, Goddard, and all of

the others had moved out of doors themselves. Worthington and two of the footmen were in the process
of hastily setting up the outdoor tables and chairs so
that the company could enjoy luncheon or tea or
some other refreshment in the balmy, summer air.
Even Percy, Spencer, and Clarence were there, and
Seymour had come down from the nursery to pass
some time with Septimus and the others. Every single
one of his friends was there to witness his fit of pique
as he burst out among them, Luc hard on his tail.

"Redmond, wait," Luc called out, obviously furi-
ous. He stopped as soon as he, too, noted their sudden
audience.

There was a moment of supreme awkwardness as
all of the men stared at each other. It was enough to
leave Red wondering how much of his argument with
Luc the others had overheard and if the entire purpose of moving the conversation outside so that
Haight and Goddard did not hear anything that would
have incriminated Red and Luc for being lovers.
Whatever the case, it was too late now.

"This situation calls for a game," Red called out to
the stunned assembly watching his tantrum.

He could both shift the mood of the company and
relieve the restlessness that was about to drive him
mad by expending his energy in yet another mad
game—even though it felt exactly like the endless,
repetitive cycle of his nightmares about Shaw. Games
were different, he insisted to himself as he all but ran
for the chest of sporting equipment. Games were supposed to make things better. They were supposed to
chase demons of guilt and melancholy away.

"We have more than enough men to form sides,"
he went on as he reached the chest. "Anthony, Barrett,
Spencer, you are on my side. Clarence, Septimus, Sey-

mour, Goddard, you can form the other side." Red was careful not to mention Luc's name at all.

"I wish to be on Mr. Goddard's team," Percy said, leaping up from the seat where he'd taken up a pose of leisure and had been making eyes at poor Goddard.

"I...er...I am not dressed for any sort of sporting activity," Goddard protested.

"Neither are the rest of us, darling," Percy said, grasping Goddard's arm and lifting him out of his chair. "That is what makes impromptu games such as this one so scintillating."

Deep in the recesses of Red's mind that had been shut off by the pain that roiled through him, part of him wanted to laugh at the torment Percy was likely deliberately inflicting on Goddard. Goddard was like a mouse that Percy's cat was enjoying playing with before either devouring it or letting it go. There was also a fair chance that Percy was engaging in silly antics to counter the alarm that the rest of the company seemed to be filled with over Red's behavior.

"What game are we playing?" Barrett asked, striding swiftly down the slope of the hill so that he was at Red's side when Red reached the chest. In a quieter voice he said, "Or rather, I should ask what game are you playing."

"No game at all." Red threw open the top of the chest, reaching inside to pull out mallets and tossing them to the grass as though he were laying out battle axes for a coming war. "I merely cannot stand the thought of stillness for another moment. Not when everything else is moving around me and Luc is on the verge of sailing away to India." His voice nearly cracked at those last words.

Barrett let out a heavy breath and shoved a hand through his hair. "You need to stop this childishness at once and admit that you love the man and you want him with you."

"I need to admit nothing of the sort," Red growled in return. He contradicted himself somewhat when he straightened and glanced around to see if Luc was near enough to hear his conversation with Barrett. And when his heart squeezed in his chest when he found that Luc had not followed him, for once. He'd stayed nearer the top of the slope, discussing something quietly with Anthony. Discussing him, likely.

For some reason, that made the pain deep within Red burn. "He'll do well without me," he growled, thrusting mallets at those of his friends—like Clarence and Septimus—who had dared to come near him. They were treating him as though he were some wild animal on the verge of escaping his cage.

"Red, you are unwell," Barrett said in a commanding voice, closing his hand around Red's wrist once he'd grabbed a mallet for himself. "You need calm and you need tranquility. We all know that these last several months have been a trial for you, that Shaw's death—"

"What I need is for you to leave me bloody well alone," he shouted, yanking away from Barrett. "What I need is to run and to use my body, to play this game, and to win it."

He didn't wait for Barrett to argue with him further. Inside, he felt as though he were on fire and as if the embers would reduce him to a snapping, agitated pile of charcoal. He refused to admit that he was close to tears or that the anguish he hadn't been able to escape, even in his dreams, made him feel as though he were dancing on a knife's edge of sanity. And he refused most of all to let himself believe that Luc's imminent departure would destroy him.

"We shall keep this game simple," he told the others, smacking his mallet into a ball that he'd tossed out of the chest earlier. "That end of the lawn is the goal of my team. This end of the lawn is the goal for the other. The ball will start in the middle of the field, and using the mallets alone, whichever team hits their ball to the markers on their side of the field wins."

It was crude as far as rules went. He hadn't defined the markers that each side needed to hit the ball past. They should have set up wickets or stumps and bales, or anything to make the goal clearer. The only goal that Red had was to run, to feel sweat soak his shirt and his brow, and to hit something. Hard. He bristled with the need to smash things, to tear down and break the world of pain that had built up within him since Shaw's death and that would not let him go. Perhaps if he could crush that, the world would see just how destructive he was and how he did not deserve their friendship or their love.

He did not deserve Luc's love. Not when a sweet and lively soul like Shaw would never have the chance to know love at all. Not when thousands of men had been blown to bits, leaving bereft lovers utterly alone.

"Does no one on your side dare to face me?" he demanded of the players on what he assumed was the other side as they milled around the edge of the field, whispering to each other and making anxious gestures toward him. "Come on and play! Surely one of you must be better than a coward."

Too many parts of him cried out for caution within him, begging him to stop being such an arse and to listen to reason for a change. He couldn't, though. Things had gone too far beyond that, and if he didn't rage, he would weep. And once he started weeping, he didn't think he would ever be able to stop.

Finally, the others took up wary positions on the field. It was clear as day to Red that none of them wished to play, but that they were humoring him. Unsurprisingly, Luc was the one who marched out into the center of the field to face him.

"Very well," he said, holding his arms wide, a mallet in one hand. "Tell me what you wish me to do. Tell me the rules of your game and I will follow them."

Inwardly, Red winced. Luc had only ever given him everything. The man only wanted to help him. But Red could not allow it. The pain within him was too great, and if he failed to keep him at arm's length, that pain would destroy Luc as well.

Red tapped the ball on the grass between them with the head of his mallet. "We each take a few steps back, and on the count of three, we run forward to hit the ball. The first one of us to send the ball across the opposing side of the field wins."

"Very well," Luc said with a resigned look. He took several steps back when Red did, grasping his mallet in both hands. "Whatever you need to exorcise this anger, I will play along."

Red's heart squeezed in his chest, but he glared at Luc as though his friend had issued the very worst of insults. "I do not need your pity," he growled.

"It is not pity, Red," Luc said with a weary sigh. "I only wish for you to be well again in mind and body. Because I love you."

Red's throat closed up, and the urge to fall apart was so great that he tensed every muscle in his body to counteract the feeling. He could not give into it. He could not fall to pieces simply because the man he loved more than life itself had laid his heart on the line when Red was behaving at his very worst.

"I will win this game," he growled instead,

clenching his mallet hard. "On the count of three." Luc nodded, staring straight into his eyes with a deadly combination of love and sorrow. It set Red's teeth on edge and paradoxically made his temper flare. "One," he began, "two, three."

The two of them charged for the ball, Red's teeth bared in a rictus. As soon as he was close, Red put every bit of strength he possessed into smashing the pall-mall ball has hard as he could, letting out a cry of rage for every horrific loss he'd witnessed during the war and for the precious life that had been ended because of his negligence. That rage gave him power he didn't know he had.

But he missed the ball. Instead, the head of his mallet brushed the top of the ball and went crashing into Luc's shin, causing a sickening snap as Luc's leg buckled unnaturally.

A moment later, Luc let out a howl of pain like nothing Red had ever heard before and tumbled to the grass.

10

There was a moment directly after the impact when everything went distant and fuzzy for Luc. He heard the crack and he felt the bizarre sensation of his leg not quite being as it should be, but it took another strange, unreal second before the pain hit him. But once it hit him, it was like nothing he'd ever experienced before.

He let out an unmanly roar of agony as he tumbled to the grass, his weight no longer supported by his injured leg. His roaring didn't stop as the pain increased in intensity, enveloping his entire leg, not just his shin bone. He grasped at his leg, rocking and writhing and unable to stay still and unable to alleviate the torture in the slightest.

"Luc," Red called out, throwing aside his mallet and diving to the grass by Luc's side. "My God, Luc, I am so sorry."

Red threw his arms around Luc's shoulders for a moment, but when Luc flinched with pain and cried out again, he jerked back, his eyes going wide.

"I did not mean to hurt you," Red gulped. "Truly, I did not."

He then did something Luc had never seen him

do. He burst into sobs, hunching in on himself and curling forward as though he might be sick. The sound of his sorrow was so loud and fierce that it shocked Luc out of his pain for the briefest of moments. He'd wanted Red to open himself to the guilt that had trapped him since arriving at Wodehouse Abbey, but of all times for that to happen.…

"Dear God, is it broken?" Anthony thundered as he, Barrett, and Spencer ran over to assess what had happened.

The shift in focus away from Red and back to Luc's injury somehow made his pain double. He cried out and shifted his whole body again, desperate to find a position that didn't make him feel as though his leg was a gateway to Hell itself.

"I broke it," Red wailed in answer, his face red and shining with sweat and tears. "I smashed his shin with my mallet, and.…" Whatever else he could have said was drown by a fit of sudden hysterics. Those hysterics ended with Red heaving up the contents of his stomach onto the grass.

"Someone rush into Hull to find a doctor at once," Anthony boomed, straightening and giving orders to whoever would hear him. "In the meantime, Worthington, does Mrs. Miniver, the bonesetter, still live with the tenants on the estate."

"I believe so, Your Grace," Worthington replied quickly, already jogging toward the cluster of footmen at the top of the yard as he went on with, "I'll send for her immediately."

Anthony nodded, then glanced to Barrett and Spencer, and now Septimus, who had joined them as well. "We need to move Lucas somewhere safe and more comfortable."

"No! Do not move him," Sigglesthorpe called out,

joining the group, Clarence right behind him. "He must stay right where he is and move as little as possible."

"He's in the middle of an open field," Anthony protested, though he didn't look entirely certain of his assessment. "He should be taken to shelter."

Sigglesthorpe shook his head and insisted in a surprisingly commanding voice for a dandy, "His leg needs to be kept completely stationary. It does not appear as though the bone has broken clean through, but if it is danger of doing so, if the muscles around it are allowed to contract at all, then whatever distress Mr. Salterford is in now will seem like a child's game compared to what could happen."

"And just how do you know so much about bones?" Clarence asked him, looking impressed in spite of the tension of the moment.

Sigglesthorpe straightened, then rested his weight on one hip before saying, "Young man, are you asking me how I know about *bones*?" turning the serious moment into a joke.

In spite of everything, Luc burst into laughter. He needed that momentary diversion. But it only lasted a moment. His pain flared again as Barrett accidentally touched him while attempting to step around and check on Red. He hadn't even jostled Luc's injured leg, but his entire body seemed to have become a lightning rod for agony.

As soon as he voiced his pain, Red groaned as well. "I'm sorry, I am so sorry," he moaned, reaching for Luc, but drawing back at the last minute, as though he didn't feel he had the right to touch him. When Barrett knelt by his side and attempted to rest a hand on Red's shoulder, Red batted him away.

"Give him this," Mr. Haight's steady voice cut

through the swirling panic that surrounded Luc. Spencer and Septimus stepped aside to allow the man through. He held a decanter of port that he must have taken from the house. "It's crude medicine, but if Mr. Salterford can stomach it, it might do well to numb the pain."

Luc had never been much of a port drinker. He preferred rum or gin or the other quick and dirty spirits that sailors craved. But under the circumstances, he had no room to be picky. He grabbed the decanter from Haight, threw aside the stopper, and downed as much of the sickly-sweet liquid as he could.

When he felt he might cast up what he'd already swallowed, he pushed the decanter toward Red. "Give him some too," he said in a hoarse voice.

"No." Red shook his head. "I do not deserve it. I am the one who caused this disaster. I should face it as I am."

Luc's patience was as brittle as icicles because of the pain. He glared at Red, holding the decanter out with a badly-shaking hand. "Drink some, by God, or I will smash you over the head with this to see if your skull breaks as easily as my shin."

A moment of stunned silence followed as the others gaped, seemingly unsure whether they should laugh or not. Red's face pinched with misery for a moment before he took the decanter with hands shaking as violently as Luc's and downed a few gulps.

"Now," Luc said, gasping and desperate for a breath that did not send knives of agony through him. "Cease your hysterics and help me, man."

Luc was surprised that his command actually worked. Red nodded, took another gulp of port, then handed the decanter off to Spencer before inching toward Luc.

"I need someone to lean against," Luc panted, meeting Red's eyes. "Shore me up from behind, because I don't think I have the strength—"

He didn't need to finish his sentence. Red was behind him, sitting straight so that Luc could lean his weight against him. It was clear to Luc that his lover was still stunned and bereft with guilt, but for the first time in days, Red's turmoil was the very least of Luc's problems.

"Should we remove his shoe and possibly his hose and breeches to get a look at the leg itself?" Anthony asked no one in particular.

"It might be wise," Barrett said. "We'll probably have to cut his breeches to expose his leg."

"Do whatever needs to be done," Luc gulped and nodded through the pain.

He sat as steadily as he could for the next several minutes as his friends gingerly removed his shoe and stocking while attempting not to move his leg. A footman brought a heavy pair of shears from the house with which to cut his breeches. The sight that met them all when Luc's shin was exposed was enough to cause Luc to swoon. Even through the skin and muscle, it was clear that the bone had been snapped. Where there had once been a smooth, defined line to mark his shin bone, there was now a decided dent. The top and bottom of his bone no longer aligned perfectly. The difference was subtle and not so bad that he felt his leg muscles were in danger of contracting and thrusting the bone clear through the skin —a thought which made him nauseated merely imagining it—but Luc could feel how precarious the situation was. It took every bit of strength he had left to stay as still as possible and to will his bone not to slip into catastrophe.

Luc was surprised when, within an hour, one of the footmen came charging up from the far side of the estate with a large woman. The woman carried a long satchel with her, and as she and the footman reached the group surrounding Luc on the lawn, without greeting or showing any deference to the lords in her presence, she went straight toward Luc.

"How was this done?" she asked without preamble as she squatted beside Luc.

The others took a step back, except for Red, who stayed propped against Luc's back. Luc's strength had waned with pain and as he'd managed to drink more port, but he still had enough presence of mind to say, "I was hit with a pall-mall mallet. A direct hit."

The woman—who could only have been Mrs. Miniver—hummed and nodded, then gingerly rested a hand over the ugly bruise that had formed around Luc's bone. "Direct break," she said, almost to herself. "Not all the way through? Probably some chipping. At least the muscle hasn't contracted."

"What can he do?" Anthony asked.

"It will need to be bound and held still," Mrs. Miniver said, giving no indication she was speaking to a duke. "I need to make certain the bone truly is set. You'll want to hold him down for that part."

Luc gulped at her ominous words but nodded. He knew what had to be done.

The next few minutes were excruciating as Mrs. Miniver pulled and shoved at Luc's leg, slipping the bone as much into its former position as she could. Red continued to shore him up from behind, but Luc felt him trembling the whole time. The others had to clamp him in place, and indeed, it took the full strength of the burliest among them, Clarence and Septimus, to stop Luc from thrashing and flailing as Mrs. Miniver did her work. It was too much for him, and for a moment, Luc passed out.

When he regained consciousness what could only have been a few minutes later, he was lying on his back in the grass with a heavy splint of some sort clamped to his leg.

"The doctor might try to say something different," Mrs. Miniver was telling Anthony and an extraordinarily pale Red above where Luc lay, "but he don't know as much about bones as I do. It will heal just fine, but he'll probably have a limp for the rest of his days."

Luc blinked at the prediction, then let out a breath and closed his eyes for a moment. It hadn't been that bad, had it? But like Mrs. Miniver had said, she knew more about bones than even a doctor.

"Can we move him up to the house now?" Anthony asked.

"Aye, you can," Mrs. Miniver said with a nod, though she didn't sound pleased. "Just be careful about it. It'd be best if you had a chair or even a board to lay him on while you move him."

"Fetch one at once," Anthony ordered.

Luc was treated to a whole new round of pain and indignation as two of the Abbey's footmen came down from the house with what appeared to be a door that had been swiftly taken off its hinges. Luc found the whole thing extreme, but once his friends had lifted him onto the door and carried him back to the house, he reassessed the plan. It truly was the best way to convey him into the house, and even then, every small jostle was agony.

By the time Luc was settled on a settee in one of

the parlors and as comfortable as it was possible for him to be with a shattered leg, the doctor from Hull had arrived. There was a bit of a battle of wills as Mrs. Miniver and Dr. Norris stared each other down and debated the skill and efficacy of the splint Mrs. Miniver had fastened to Luc's leg, but in the end, the doctor was forced to concede that Mrs. Miniver had done fine work and that her advice to keep the leg perfectly still and bound was the best that could have been done.

"You seem well otherwise," Dr. Norris said after doing a quick inspection of Luc's body. "You are young, which works to your advantage. Your body should heal quickly."

"How quickly?" Luc asked, a sinking feeling forming in his stomach.

Dr. Norris made a noncommittal gesture. "Breaks like this require weeks to heal, months sometimes. I would advise that you stay off your feet for six weeks at a minimum. I advise bed rest and laudanum to manage the pain."

"For six weeks?" Anthony asked, as though Luc's care was now his responsibility, and as if he intended to take that responsibility seriously.

"Yes, Your Grace." Dr. Norris suddenly turned all of his attention to Anthony, treating Luc as though he were a bit of furniture instead of the one who was injured. "He should remain as still as possible and be given as much bone broth and other fortifying nourishment as possible."

"Is it true that he'll walk with a limp once he's healed?" Barrett asked, his brow knit in concern.

Dr. Norris glanced flatly at Mrs. Miniver—who stood straighter and crossed her arms over her ample chest, as though daring the doctor to contradict her—

then sighed. "Most patients with this sort of break in a leg bone walk with a limp to some degree, yes," he said.

Luc swallowed and sank back against the settee, letting the implication of those words wash over him while the conversation continued. It was distressing to think that he would be impaired that way for the rest of his days, though there were plenty of men of his acquaintance with just a small limp who managed to lead active lives. Some had even retained the ability to run and engage in sporting contests.

More distressing was the time it would take for him to recover. The Admiralty wanted him in Portsmouth in a week's time, to captain a ship that was set to depart in a month. He would not be hale and hearty in time. He might never be fit enough to captain a ship ever again. With so many recently decommissioned officers champing at the bit for a command after the war, his chances of ever receiving another commission and returning to a career as a naval officer had all but disappeared.

The conversation with Dr. Norris and Mrs. Miniver ended and the two departed while Luc was caught up in his thoughts. As there was nothing more his friends could do, most of them returned to the lawn to pack away the mallets that had been taken out for the ill-fated game or to expend their anxious energy in some other way, or so Luc assumed. What came as no surprise to him was that Red remained in the parlor, along with the footman who had been directed to rearrange the parlor for Luc's comfort. Red sat on the end of the settee, his shoulders hunched and his face pale and drawn.

When he noticed that the others were gone, Red sent Luc a mournful look and said, "This is all my—"

"So help me God, Redmond," Luc cut him off, impatient and dizzy from port and the initial dose of laudanum Dr. Norris had given him, "if you blame yourself for this, broken leg or no, I will tear off this splint and thrash you with it."

Red's eyes turned glassy and his expression twisted. "How can you view me as anything other than a devil after everything I've done?"

"You are not the inventor of frustration, nor are you the first man to vent your anger and guilt in violent ways," Luc said at him, biting his words.

"I did not mean to hurt you," Red told him, an edge of desperation to his words. "I have never meant to hurt you. Not ever. You mean far too much to me." His mouth hung open, and for a moment, Luc half expected the confession that he'd longed to hear from Red's lips for years. Red snapped his mouth shut and shook his head, though. "I've ruined everything. I ruin everything and everyone wherever I go."

"You do not, and I would thank you to stop clobbering yourself over everything."

Red jerked to stare, wide-eyed, at Luc over the force in his words. "You, of all people, should know how unworthy I am of any sort of compassion or consideration."

Luc let out a heavy breath and closed his eyes, rubbing his forehead as the laudanum had a greater and greater effect on him. "You are a man, Red. You are no more of a devil or a saint than any other man. You take things too much to heart, and you always have. I love the tenderness and openness of your heart—" there seemed to be no point in holding back his feelings for Red now, "—but do not let the openness of your heart transform into the disease of melancholia. Spirits are much harder to mend than bones."

He wasn't certain his words made sense as his head filled up with cotton-wool, but his heart felt as though it had spoken correctly.

"Luc," Red breathed his name softly, "if you can find a way to forgive me—"

He stopped when he accidentally bumped Luc's foot while inching toward him and when Luc winced and moaned in pain. That was enough to send Red leaping off the settee.

"I cannot," he said, distress straining his voice. "I cannot inflict any more pain on you than I already have. You are better off without me."

He strode for the doorway, nearly running. Luc wanted to call out and stop him, but the alcohol and the medicine had done their work, and instead of being able to tell Red he was forgiven for everything and that he was loved unconditionally, Luc fell into a heavy slumber.

11

R ed shot across the hall, his face buried in his hands, and into the morning parlor, which was now dim because of the angle of the sun. The feeling that his insides, his pain, was too big to be contained by his body and that he might burst out of his skin entirely was worse than ever. It had grown far beyond the normal realms of guilt and disappointment that he'd felt for himself since the accident on the *Majesty*. Everything that had just happened to Luc was proof that his utter inadequacy as a man wasn't a single incident, it was becoming a pattern.

He'd fought for weeks to hide his misery behind games and activities, jokes and laughter, but it all came crashing down on him now. He threw himself onto one of the sofas in the morning parlor, burying his face against the back of the seat in the crook of his arm and wept. The gesture was horrifically unbecoming and unmanly, but he could no longer keep the darkness inside. He was a disgrace in every conceivable way, and he deserved to feel humiliated for it. The pain that lashed him was nothing to the pain he'd inflicted on Luc, and even that, as horrible as it was, could not hold a candle to Shaw's death and the deaths of every other man in the war.

He should be cast out of society altogether. Men like him did not deserve to be in the company of good people. Red felt that as truth deep within his soul, beyond the reach of reason and sense. There was an infinitesimally small part of his mind that whispered forgiveness and hinted that he was not feeling like himself and that perhaps he should have heeded Luc's pleas to discuss what had happened with Shaw instead of letting the darkness build within him. But the darkness itself reared up and swallowed that tiny, sane voice, roaring that he didn't deserve any sort of consideration at all. That beast within him suggested that perhaps he didn't even deserve his life anymore. Why should he live when so many better men had died senselessly?

"Redmond, are you well?"

Red snapped straight and gulped as Anthony appeared in the doorway behind him. He twisted to face his brother as though he were an animal that Anthony had cornered and wished to exterminate.

"You are not well," Anthony said without waiting for a response, moving deeper into the room. "You are not well at all, and I should have seen it much sooner." He made a scolding sound and shook his head.

"I am perfectly fine." Red leapt up from the sofa and paced away from his brother, loath to have Anthony see the tears and sweat that stained his face. He wiped them with the back of his sleeve as best he could, but feared it only made him look worse.

"You are not fine by any stretch of the imagination." Anthony followed him, a gentle compassion in his voice that Red hadn't heard since he was a boy and Anthony was charged with taking care of him. "You have clearly been distressed for quite some time, but I failed to recognize as much and act upon it in the way a brother should have."

"It's nothing," Red hissed when Anthony all but cornered him by one of the windows. "I feel guilty for breaking Luc's leg and causing him pain. It was a rash and despicable thing to do, even if it was an unintentional slip, a momentary lapse of concentration. I let my temper get the better of me, and now Luc is gravely injured."

Anthony didn't rush to either agree with him or contradict him. He stood where he was, studying Red for a long time, his brow knit in concern. At last, he took in a long, slow breath and said, "You love him."

It wasn't a question, but Red's instincts were to deny it. He even opened his mouth to spout the denial, but he couldn't.

"I have no right to love a man as good and kind and generous as Lucas Salterford," he said on a heavy sigh.

Again, Anthony neither agreed with him nor contradicted him. "Why do you believe that?" he asked.

The anger, shame, and heartbreak within Red reared up once again. "Because Luc is the most competent man I've ever known, and the jolliest. He gathers friends and respect wherever he goes. Our superiors adored him, and those who served under him on the *Hawk* admired him like no other officer, not even his captain. He is fair and generous, and he is the most fantastic lover I've ever lain with." His words grew faster the more he spoke, and he finally burst out at the end with, "He never would have allowed Shaw to play in the rigging or to fall to his death because of it."

He turned away from Anthony as soon as he'd finished and glared out through the window over the side garden.

"Is that what has troubled you so much since your arrival?" Anthony asked, taking another step toward him. "Midshipman Shaw's death?"

Every fiber and sinew of Red's body wanted to flee. He did not want to talk about his failures and his shame, particularly not to his older brother, the man he'd looked up to for his entire life. If Anthony knew the truth, he would be disgusted. He would push Red away. But that quiet voice in his head that believed Luc was right, that he needed to speak of the matter to someone, somehow managed to override that louder roar that insisted he did not deserve Anthony's approval.

He turned to Anthony, leaning heavily against the wall beside the window. "Shaw died on my watch because I was not strong enough to order the boys to stop playing and come down from the rigging."

Anthony crossed his arms and frowned. The posture made him look so much like a judge about to sentence him to death that it sent a chill down Red's spine. "Did the midshipmen climb the rigging frequently?" he asked.

Red took a moment to answer him. He swallowed hard, anticipating where the question would lead. "They liked to, yes," he said. "But Captain Wallace was adamant that they only climb the rigging with supervision, and only when they had a specific task they were meant to accomplish."

"And were they supervised?" Anthony asked. "Were they up there to complete a task?"

Red stared at a blank point on the opposite wall, wracking his memory for the answer to Anthony's question and coming up short. The trouble was, he couldn't remember. Everything from that afternoon was blurred. Besides which, his nightmares showed him a different scenario every time he closed his eyes. He didn't know where dreams ended and reality began anymore. If he could just remember, maybe the truth would set him free.

He shook his head before focusing on Anthony again. "The younger midshipmen, like Shaw, rarely had reason to climb the rigging. Rigging and sails, everything above the decks, is the province of the boatswain. Older midshipmen might sometimes supervise the handling of the sails, but not aboard the *Majesty*. The whole point of the rank of midshipman is to train young men who will one day become officers in the duties of an officer, not to have them perform the tasks of common seamen."

"But they do sometimes oversee handling of sails," Anthony said as though puzzling the whole thing out. "And it is their duty to learn everything possible about the tasks aboard ship so that one day they might command."

"Yes," Red said frowning.

"Is that what the *Majesty's* midshipmen were doing on the day Shaw died?" Anthony asked. "Were they learning something pertinent to seamanship?"

Red shook his head, then shrugged. "We knew the war was over and that we would be returning to England soon. Discipline aboard was lax. The boys were playing."

"And were they the only ones in the rigging?"

Red let out an impatient breath and pushed away from the wall, desperate to get away from Anthony. "I know what you are doing, and it is futile. The accident was my fault. I was responsible for the death of a man who never truly had a chance to live. And now I have likely crippled a good man who does not deserve it."

"You have hurt someone you love," Anthony reframed the statement.

"I do not," Red snapped back to him when he reached the far end of the room. "Luc is a friend only. Fucking is not love."

Anthony pursed his lips and narrowed his eyes at Red as he came to a stop in the middle of the room. "You do yourself a great disservice by denying your feelings for the man," he insisted.

"I do him a great disservice by having those feelings to begin with," Red threw back in return. He realized after the fact that he had as much as admitted to Anthony that he was in love.

Anthony flexed his jaw for a moment before saying, "Were you not the very man who stood in this room only a few weeks ago, insisting to me that there was nothing wrong or evil about me pursuing my unfolding feelings for Barrett?"

"I was." Red took a step toward him. "But have never run from my baser instincts, atypical as they are. I accept that I desire men and not women."

"But you refuse to accept that you are in love with a particular man, and that he is in love with you," Anthony argued. "And believe me, it is obvious to one and all, and has been since he stepped foot in this house, that Lucas Salterford is deeply in love with you."

"He should not be." Red pivoted to face away from him, but the gesture pointed him to the doorway. He could see across the wide front hall and into the afternoon parlor, where Luc was laid out, unable to get up and walk away from whatever he might be overhearing.

"As I have come to see," Anthony said, a sigh in his voice, "there is no 'should' in love. One simply loves, whether there is any rhyme or reason to the emotion or not. You cannot escape it any more than Lucas can."

"I do not deserve to be loved," Red spat, turning back to Anthony. "I do not deserve anything so free or so tender. Not when I have proven myself to be the very worst of characters. Not when better men than me had their lives cut short."

Anthony merely frowned at him in response, as if working even harder to puzzle out the mystery of Red's character. "I do not recall you expressing sentiments like this before you accepted your commission and went off to the war."

"That is because war changes a man," Red spat. He took a few more steps toward Anthony so that he could keep his voice down, in case Luc truly could hear him. "War is hardship. It is harsh. I left here a carefree trickster, but I soon learned about discipline aboard ship. I learned what it was to see men whipped for disobeying orders so that an example could be set and discipline maintained. I learned the consequences of disobedience and negligence of duty."

He paused for a moment as sour memories of his service rushed back in on him, as if every memory wanted to be remembered at once.

"I know what it looks like when a man is blown apart by cannon fire, even though he was the enemy and he would have killed me, if given half a chance. I know that persistent cannon fire sound like thunder that is part of a never-ending storm. I have heard the screams and shouts of men who know they are doomed, and I have questioned whether the cause we were fighting and killing and dying for was truly a just one. But then all of that was over." He lifted his shoulders in a helpless shrug. "The war was over, and we were all going home. Those of us who were lucky enough to survive the carnage could put all of that aside and move on with our lives."

He turned away from Anthony again, unable to hide the guilt that pinched his face and threatened to have him in tears again. "We were all so ready to return home," he whispered, "but Shaw was never given that boon. And it was entirely my fault. He was my responsibility."

"Everything comes back to that boy," Anthony said with a helpless sigh. "That I can understand. What I do not understand is why you persistently deny yourself comfort from the one man who understands that best. Why do you turn away from him when all of us can see he wishes nothing more than to embrace you and ease you through this new war you are fighting?"

Red whipped back to face his brother. "Luc does not deserve to be burdened by someone like me."

"Yes, he does not deserve a peevish and arrogant bastard who would injure him, possibly permanently, and who would then turn his back on him," Anthony said, raising his voice. He lowered it again to say, "He deserves the strong, vibrant trickster that you have always been. He deserves the man who cares so deeply about his fellow men that he would tear his soul to shreds for them."

Red flinched at his brother's surprising appraisal. "He can do better."

"So can you," Anthony insisted. He closed the distance between him, resting a heavy hand on Red's shoulders. "You are better than this, Red. You are not a coward, and you never have been. I can see that it is difficult for you to accept that this man might just love you in spite of the things you see as flaws in your character. I never would have imagined that you would be so needlessly cruel to someone you care about so deeply."

"I am not—"

"And now your friend needs you more than ever," Anthony cut off his protest. "The poor man lies injured in the other room. He will not be able to care for himself or tend to his own needs for weeks. And yes, that is your doing."

"I feel so ashamed," Red burst out before he could stop himself. He jerked his head away from Anthony, but Anthony wouldn't release his shoulder, no matter how hard Red squirmed.

"You behaved like an arse," Anthony agreed. "Your fit of spleen was disgraceful, yes. But I am beginning to wonder if the fault for that does not fall on all of our shoulders. We should have seen your suffering sooner and helped you."

Red gaped at him. "It is not your fault that I could not control my temper and that I smashed Luc's leg with a mallet."

"No?" Anthony let go of him and leaned back. "Are you saying that a man's actions are his own, even when they are inadvisable and cause harm, and that the others around him who should have had a care for his person are not accountable for any accidents that happen?"

Red's mouth dropped, and his gut filled with anger. How dare Anthony attempt to turn the tables on him? Anthony didn't understand a single thing about the agony he had lived in every day since Shaw's death.

And yet, that quiet voice of sense that still existed deep within him whispered that Anthony was right. As much as all mankind all bore a degree of responsibility for each other in this life, they could not cast blame around every time Fate played a cruel joke.

"I refuse to stay here and listen to this," he said, unwilling to embrace his own reason.

He pivoted to leave, but Anthony caught him and held him to his spot.

"You can listen to me or flee all you'd like," he said, "but the fact remains that your dearest friend, your lover, has been badly hurt. He is in need of care. Practical care. He will be for weeks. Whether you lash yourself with blame and wish to punish yourself for a momentary lapse of sense or whether you choose to look deep into yourself and forgive everything you've done, you have a responsibility to that man."

"I—" Red tried to protest, but he knew his brother was right.

"You will tend to Lucas's every need as he recovers," Anthony ordered him. And it was an order, there was no mistaking that. "You will assist him with dressing and moving, pissing and bathing. You will fetch and carry for him, and you will feed him if he cannot feed himself. In short, you will be that man's servant until he has fully recovered." He paused, leaning back, then added, "Consider that your penance and perform it well."

Red was stunned speechless by his brother's command. The thought of staying glued to Luc's side, of watching every grimace of pain and every indignity that Luc was certain to suffer because of his rashness felt akin to torture. On the other hand, that sort of torture might be exactly what he deserved. He should not be happy or comfortable as long as Luc was suffering, because he was the cause of that suffering.

"Alright," he said weakly, stepping away from Anthony. "I'll do it. It's only fair. I was the cause of this misery, therefore I should be the solution to it."

"Finally, a word of sense from you," Anthony said, the barest hint of a smile pulling at the corners of his mouth. "I will tell Worthington that you will be solely responsible for Lucas's care as he recovers."

Red's gut squeezed with the implications of what he was about to undertake. It terrified him. He didn't believe he was up to the task for so many reasons. But the absolute discomfort of what he was about to do was exactly what he deserved.

"Now," Anthony went on, shifting his stance and gazing on Red with more compassion than before, "I suggest you inspect Lucas's guest room to make certain it has every convenience an invalid will need for the next few weeks. If it lacks for anything, I suggest you remedy that. And when you're done with all that, I think it would be wise for you figure out a way to convey your friend to his room, because he may end up spending a great deal of time there in the next few weeks."

Red sighed and pressed his fingertips to his temples. "You're right," he said. "That is what I should do."

He turned to go, but Anthony stopped him after only a few steps with, "Redmond, have a care for yourself as well." He crossed the room to pull Red into a brotherly embrace.

It felt so good to have his brother's strong arms around him that Red had to swallow the lump that came to his throat and gather his wits again before he could straighten. "I will, Tony," he said, attempting to smile.

But as he turned away and set to work on the tasks Anthony had set before him, he wasn't certain how he was supposed to care for or forgive himself ever again.

12

L uc was uncertain how much time he'd spent
floating in a haze of laudanum-soaked pain, immobile and, for the most part, insensible. He'd been
moved up to his guestroom without any awareness of
the process, and he was reasonably certain that he'd
spend more than one day being monitored, soothed,
fed, and dosed with more laudanum until the worst of
the initial pain had passed. What puzzled his addled
mind was the distinct impression that Red, not one of
the footmen, or even Dr. Norris, had been the one
caring for his every need.

When he finally blinked awake, feeling for the first
time in ages that he was not simply moving from one
dream into another, he found himself in bed with a
mountain of pillows propped behind him. Late-
morning sunlight streamed in through the open windows on one side of his room. His bedchamber was on
the side of the house that faced the sea, and even
though it was over a mile away, a pleasant, tangy
breeze billowed the curtains and filled the room with
the fresh, familiar feeling of the ocean.

Luc breathed it in, glad that his head had finally
cleared, and he was willing to endure a bit of pain in

his leg to feel that way. He adjusted the way he reclined, using his arms to push up straighter, then threw aside the light blanket covering the lower half of his body to get a look at his injury. Someone had dressed him in his nightshirt while he'd been insensible, which was probably for the best, and all he needed to do was tug it up a bit to see the bulky, ugly splint that was fastened to his right leg below the knee.

He tried flexing his toes, and though it was possible, between the stiffness of the splint and bandages and the renewed throbbing in his shin, it wasn't worth it.

"Bugger," he growled, easing back on the cushions and glaring at his leg as though it were a traitor.

His exclamation caused a rush of movement on the other side of the room. Luc flinched and glanced over to see Red sitting in a chair by the empty fireplace. He had one elbow rested on the chair's arm, and judging by the way he jerked and blinked, bleary-eyed, as he sat straighter, Luc's expletive had woken him from an awkward nap.

"You're awake," Red mumbled, standing and brushing the front of his wrinkled waistcoat, then tugging at his sleeves. His jacket was draped over the back of the chair, but the rest of Red was so creased that Luc wondered if it, and Red, had been there for days.

"I was about to say the same thing to you," Luc said. His throat felt rough and dry from disuse.

"It was just a short nap," Red said, stepping toward the side of Luc's bed. He seemed to look at everything except Luc's face.

"How long have I been in a laudanum-induced stupor?" Luc asked, shifting again in an attempt to find a more comfortable position.

Red leapt to rearrange the pillows behind him, helping him to a more upright position. At first, Luc smiled at the friendly proximity between the two of them. He would never complain about being close to Red. Judging by the scent, neither of them had bathed or been bathed in days, but Luc had always felt comforted by the scent of Red's body. Even when it was rank. Conditions had been much worse, at times, when they were aboard one of their ships or on shore leave.

He was so caught up in those pleasant thoughts that it took him a moment to realize Red hadn't replied. He seemed furiously intent on his task of making Luc comfortable, and even after Luc was settled, Red lingered before pulling away.

"It's only been two days," he said in an exhausted, hollow voice. "We would have given you more time to avoid the pain, but we ran out of laudanum."

"No, no," Luc raised a hand, laughing slightly. "I'm glad that part is over. I don't think I like the stuff. I'd rather suffer a little and be sensible than stay in that morass."

Red's face pinched with emotion for half a second before he schooled it to neutrality. Luc had the brief impression that he would start in on another round of tearful apologies and heart-rending, but instead, he cleared his throat and said, "I would imagine you'd like some water."

"Yes, I would." Luc was relieved to have Red fetch him a glass that was already waiting on a table that had been installed in his room at some point in the last few days. He drank it gratefully but slowly, uncertain whether rushing things would make him ill.

What bothered him more was the fussy, tight way

Red went about straightening everything around Luc without meeting his eyes.

"Is everything alright, Red?" Luc asked once he'd finished his water.

Red might not have been willing to look directly at him, but he knew the instant Luc lowered the glass from his lips and came to fetch it. He also surprised Luc by saying in a quiet voice, "No, everything is not alright. You are laid up like an invalid because of my violent temper."

Luc pressed his lips together and stared at Red's back as he fled to the table to return the glass, then to fiddle with a tea set that waited there. He'd expected Red to continue to blame himself, but not in the quiet, resigned manner he was currently displaying.

"It could just as easily have been me cracking your shin," Luc said, pushing the blanket over him further aside so that he could enjoy the breeze on his un-splinted leg.

Red let out a bark of a laugh and shook his head. "No, Luc," he said, turning back to the bed with a pretty teacup in his slightly-trembling hand. "You would never have let your temper get the better of you to the point where you gravely injured someone who is so dear to you that—" He stopped, then shook his head.

Luc eyed Red warily as he brought him the cup of tea. It seemed that his lover would prove more difficult to manage than his broken leg. "I do not blame you," he said, sipping the tea. It was already lukewarm, but he planned to drink it all anyhow. Red had given it to him, and he would not do anything that made Red feel any less adequate than he already thought him-self to be.

"I blame myself," Red said, sinking carefully onto the mattress on Luc's good side, eyes downcast.

"Of course you do," Luc told him finishing the rest of his tea in a few gulps. "You are Redmond Wodehouse. It is your nature to blame yourself for every infinitesimal misfortune that befalls anyone you care about."

He said it in a teasing tone, then held his breath, waiting to see if Red would realize he was being teased or if he would take it to heart.

Blessedly, Red let out a weak breath that could have been considered a laugh and dragged his doleful eyes up to meet Luc's. "You've no idea how guilty I feel."

"You are incorrect," Luc told him, then dropped the overly formal way they were addressing each other to say, "I know you, Red. I've known you for years. I know how quick to take everything on your own shoulders you are, and—" He hesitated, wondering if the timing was all wrong or if he should lay everything between them on the table. He'd already blurted his feelings to Red once...and had his leg broken for it. "And I love you for it," he said softly, charging bravely into the fray.

Instead of arguing or creating a battle out of his confession of love, Red simply lowered his head. Luc waited with baited breath for Red to say that he loved him too.

He continued to wait when Red stood and moved close, then took the empty teacup from Luc's hands. Their fingers brushed for a moment, and it felt as though the crackling embers of a cozy fire flittered between them. All too soon, though, Red moved away, turning his back yet again and taking the teacup to the table.

"I believe Dr. Norris will be by very soon to examine you," Red said, his back still to Luc. "In the meantime, I've brought up a selection of books from the library that you might be interested in. I could read one to you, or you could read it yourself. I brought a deck of playing cards and a chess set as well. And I took the liberty of acquiring some of my brother's writing paper, should you choose to write to your family to inform them of your injury."

Luc's heart felt as though it were simultaneously expanding and contracting in his chest. He loved Red so, and at the moment, the man was in more pain than he was. But he was trying. Bless him, he was trying so hard to do what he must have thought was right by Luc. It would have been better if he had merely opened his heart to Luc and shared the depth of his troubles so that the two of them could make peace with them, with Shaw's death, together.

Luc blinked and his shoulders sagged. "I think you had better bring me some writing paper and a pen," he said, suddenly remembering what his broken leg meant. Red rushed to do as he was bidden, and Luc went on with, "I need to write to the Admiralty to tell them I will not be able to take up the captaincy of the *Daphne* in a week."

Judging by the twist of guilt without a lick of surprise that hit Red's face, his lover had already concluded what Luc had just realized about his unfitness for command.

"Let me fetch you a writing desk, or at the very least a book to write on," Red said, unable to meet his eyes again.

In the end, Luc used the largest book Red had brought up as his desk while he penned a quick letter of explanation to the Admiralty. Red hovered to one side, ready to take the missive once it was finished, dry the ink, and fold it into a form suitable for the post. As it happened, Dr. Norris arrived in the middle of the operation, and while Luc was examined, Red disappeared to find the correct address for the Admiralty, and to seal Luc's letter and likely hand it over to Worthington.

"You are healing nicely," Dr. Norris declared after poking and prodding Luc's leg. He removed the splint and bandage for the examination, carefully bathing Luc's bruised skin as he did, much to Luc's relief. He even assisted Luc in bathing the rest of his body, which was equal parts embarrassing and a relief.

Red returned to the bedchamber just as Dr. Norris was refastening the splint and bandage contraption around his leg. "Ah, you look to be much stronger than I," the doctor called out, gesturing for Red to come over to the bed. "Mr. Salterford has indicated that he would like to use the chamber pot, but he cannot leave the bed and walk on his own power."

"Should he leave his bed at all?" Red asked.

Luc snorted with laughter before he could stop himself. Only Dr. Norris's presence in the room stopped him from making a joke about Red wanting to keep him in bed.

"I advise that he remain as immobile as possible for at least a fortnight," Dr. Norris said, oblivious to the crackle of sexual tension that sprang up between Luc and Red. "Some bodily processes will be easy to take care of in bed, but others necessitate the risk of moving to the chamber pot."

"In other words," Luc said, sending Red a cheeky grin, as though they were still aboard their ships, "I don't want to shit the bed."

Dr. Norris turned an interesting shade of puce. "Yes, quite."

Red looked as though he were putting every effort possible into not cracking a smile, but his eyes betrayed his amusement. "Yes, of course," he said solemnly, then cleared his throat as he crossed the room. "What is the best way to convey Mr. Salterford from the bed to the chamber pot, then?"

It took a ridiculously long amount of time for Luc to be helped across the small bedchamber to the chamber pot, which stood behind a screen in one corner of the room. Even with the tight splint on his leg, the pain of movement was enough to leave Luc sweating. Red actually was a big help as he followed Dr. Norris's instructions for supporting him.

"Allow as much of his weight to lean on you as possible," Dr. Norris said. "Be certain to grasp his waist firmly so as to provide him as much support as you can."

Even in his pained state, the feeling of Red's arm around Luc's waist was lovely. Perhaps a little too lovely. The way Red all but carried him as he shored up Luc's right side brought them into intimate contact. Luc wore only his nightshirt still, but as he and Red tangled, Red's body warm and vibrant against his, the two of them working in concert for a single goal, Luc was glad for the loose garment. It hid the way his cock perked up with interest in spite of the throbbing in his leg.

"Are you certain this is the best way to go about this task?" Red asked, his voice laced with tension, as he shuffled Luc along. Not only did he have his arm firmly around Luc's waist, their hips were flush against each other to give Luc an added bit of support. "Could he not use a chair to cross the room?"

"It is much better this way," Dr. Norris said, still oblivious. "There is far less of a chance of Mr. Salterford falling and undoing the work his body has already done to heal his wound if he has human assistance."

"If you insist," Red said through a clenched jaw.

Luc turned his head slightly to study Red's frown of concentration. "It's not all bad, Red," he teased. "Even though I know you abhor touching me."

Red sent him a look of pure murder, but the flash in his eyes belied the amusement he actually felt.

That single look gave Luc hope on a level that he would not have dared to dream of earlier. The Red he knew and loved, the trickster who knew how to enjoy himself and who fucked like a dream, was still there beneath the mountain of guilt and regret he'd let bury him. Luc was convinced he could bring the Red he loved out again, that he could love him freely and convince Red to abandon whatever was stopping him from returning that love.

Dr. Norris left them as soon as Luc had successfully made it to the chamber pot and back. His parting words were that he was satisfied with the level of care Luc would receive, and that he would return in a few days' time to monitor his progress.

"I am receiving the finest sort of care possible," Luc told Red, one eyebrow arched to let him know that he had noted just how attentively Red was caring for him once he was settled in bed. "Need I ask why I am receiving such care?"

"You are my responsibility," Red told him, fleeing to the table so that he could busy himself there.

"Red, come back here," Luc said, unwilling to settle for the cagey behavior anymore. "Leave the cold tea and invalid entertainments you've so carefully assembled where they are and come speak with me."

Red let out a breath that lowered his shoulders and had his back hunching. He did as he'd been asked, though, returning to Luc's bedside. Instead of sitting on the bed, however, he took a seat in the chair Dr. Norris had moved to the side of the bed while examining him. That actually brought him closer to Luc than if he'd sat on the end of the bed. He was so close, that Luc could reach out a hand to him.

Red stared at his hand for several long moments before reluctantly reaching for it and grasping it in his. "I do not deserve your kindness," he mumbled as Luc threaded their fingers together.

"No, you don't," Luc told him.

Red snapped his head up, looking indignant for a moment.

Luc laughed. "You cannot fool me, Redmond Wodehouse. Your show of morose guilt is just that, a show. You would not know what to do with yourself if you didn't have me to shower you with undeserved affection."

"That is...I resent...you know not of what you speak," Red grumbled, frowning.

That only made Luc laugh harder. "You've gone formal again. Which tells me you know I am right but you are unwilling to admit it."

"I have injured you in a way you may never recover from," Red told him, seemingly more upset than ever. "How you can joke about that is beyond me."

"Yes, you've injured me," Luc said, surprised at himself for being in such a lighthearted mood. Then again, any time that he spent alone with Red tended to improve his mood. "You may even have changed the course of my future," he went on, a bit more seriously.

"But the courses we chart through life change all the time. None of us know what our futures truly hold. It may be the remnants of the laudanum talking, and I may rage and rail at you if I experience the sort of withdrawal I've been told those dosed with laudanum experience, but for now, all I care about is that the two of us are finally together."

Red shook his head, pulling his hand out of Luc's and leaning back in his chair. "I do not deserve your kind opinion. I am the worst sort of person."

"What a load of tripe," Luc said, shaking his head. "And not very original either, I might add."

Again, Red snapped to look at him in indignation.

"None of us deserves each other," Luc insisted. "Friendship, *love*, is not some reward that we receive for a job well done. It is a natural state of mankind. And I do apologize, but I will persist in loving you whether you think you are worthy or not. Because I think you are worthy simply by nature of the fact that I like you. I've always liked you. I liked you before Shaw's death and I liked you after. I love you, whether you think I should or not." He paused only slightly before adding, "And do not think you can tell me what I should or should not do. You are not my commanding officer."

Red was left stunned by the speech. Luc thought he had been rather eloquent and was proud of himself. But Red's mouth hung open in complete bafflement as he stared at Luc.

"I have no idea whatsoever of what I should say in response to that," Red said at last.

"Say nothing," Luc shrugged. "I don't need to hear you say anything. I just want you near me."

"Even though I've caused so much trouble?" Red asked.

"*Because* you've caused so much trouble," Luc laughed. "God, this convalescence would be painfully dull without you to cause trouble for me." He raised his eyebrows at Red, then went on with, "Will you do that? Will you help me through this?"

"Of course," Red said, reaching for Luc's hand once more.

Luc took it, happy for the contact between them. He could see in the depths of Red's eyes, though, that he was not the only one who had a long way to go before he was healed. And a leg was much easier to heal than a heart. But if it were the last thing Luc ever did, he would be there to help Red through his pain as well.

13

R ed wasn't supposed to find enjoyment in
waiting on Luc hand and foot. It was meant to
be his penance and his punishment for every unforgivable wrong he'd committed. But as the days
stretched into a week with Luc more or less unable
to care for his most basic needs, Red took a satisfaction from the care he gave that he felt he shouldn't
have.

"Mary brought up fresh linens earlier, and I
should let her strip and change your bed herself, but I
might as well do it while you are bathing," he told Luc
as the two of them worked together to scoot Luc to the
side of the bed.

"She could change the sheets while we are downstairs," Luc suggested with a coaxing smile and one
eyebrow arched hopefully.

Red pursed his lips and retuned that goading look
with a scolding one of his own. "Transporting you
down the stairs is a dangerous endeavor," he said.

"Dr. Norris said he saw no harm in me being carried downstairs, provided one or two of the footmen
were involved and a conveyance, like that door that
was used before, was employed," Luc argued as Red

checked the splint and bandages to be certain they were fastened tightly.

"Dr. Norris does not understand how exuberant my brother's guests are or how they will tempt you into misbehaving and doing yourself harm," Red said, glancing to Luc when he was certain the splint would stay in place through the bath. The good doctor had not been pleased with Luc's request to have a full bath, but he'd given his consent after much badgering, and instructed Red to keep the splint on while Luc was in the tub, then to replace the wet supports and bandages with dry ones once the bath was over.

Red was so distracted by his thoughts that he was taken by surprise when Luc shook with laughter. "Have I said something to amuse you?" Red stared hard at him. His insides danced with reluctant joy at the sound of Luc's laughter, though.

"So you are jealous of my brother's guests who might tempt me into misbehaving, are you?" Luc teased him—and he was clearly teasing. "You wish to keep me all to yourself? Perhaps keep me in bed? Or perhaps the bath?"

Red's face flushed hot. He denied the burst of possessive lust that shot through him, and the way his cock tightened in his breeches. "Do not be ridiculous, Lucas," he said with a sigh. "You are in no fit state for any of *that* sort of activity."

"You would be surprised," Luc said, mirth still bright in his voice.

Red had just reached under Luc's arms so that he could hoist his friend to his feet. He lifted as Luc made his comment, and when Luc punctuated his words with a suggestive smile as he and Red stood eye to eye, just a few, bare inches from each other, the desire that pulsed through Red tripled.

"My leg is the part of me that was injured," Luc went on, murmuring ardently, "not another appendage."

"How can you...you should not...injuries of the sort you have affect the entire body," Red stammered, wishing the scent of Luc's body so close to his hadn't spun his head completely around.

Luc continued to chuckle as he leaned on Red and hopped to maneuver himself to the stance they usually took when Luc insisted on getting up to use the chamber pot. "Settle yourself, Red. There's no need to hoist the mainsail and fly away yet." He glanced down at the front of Red's breeches. "Although it appears you are working with a sizable mast already."

Red flushed even hotter, scrambling to find a way to walk Luc over to the tub of water that already stood beside the fireplace in which he could hide or divert attention from the growing bulge in his breeches.

"I am only here to care for you," he insisted, making himself sound like his temper was short when, in fact, Luc had unsettled him in the tenderest of ways. It would be wrong to even begin to think of his friend in the same way he had before the injury. He didn't deserve that kind of pleasure or enjoyment.

"You've always cared for me well," Luc continued to tease him with a lascivious arch of one eyebrow.

They reached the side of the tub, and Red let out an impatient sigh. "Perhaps it is a good idea for you to keep company with someone other than me and yourself today after all," he snapped. "You've grown so restless and addled without proper company that you've nothing better to do than think about things you shouldn't."

Luc laughed even louder at that. It seemed as though everything he did or said tickled Luc in some way. "You know as well as I do that the other lads have come up to visit me more than enough since I've become an invalid. And I have a long history of thinking about things that I shouldn't, particularly when you are near." He winked at Red to emphasize his point.

Red's heart squeezed, which felt as though it had the effect of rushing more blood to his cock. "You shouldn't say such things, Luc," he said, helping Luc to balance as he removed his nightshirt. "I don't deserve them."

Luc sighed as though Red was the most tedious man of his acquaintance. "If you tell me one more time that you are not worthy of my friendship or my desire—"

"I know, I know," Red cut him off before he could finish his threat. He took the discarded nightshirt from Luc, trying extraordinarily hard not to stare at Luc's exposed body. He failed in that regard miserably. In spite of being bedridden, Luc was still strong and fit. The planes and curves of his body were so familiar to Red, and yet, looking at them now, they seemed like forbidden fruit.

That didn't stop his cock from twitching with interest at the sight of Luc's half-hard prick.

"In you go," he said instead, focusing them both on the complicated task of getting Luc into the tub.

It was enough of a challenge that the two of them forgot their banter and set aside the tension between them. For a hale and hearty man, stepping into a large brass tub and sitting was nothing. For a man with a splint and bandage on his leg, it was an exercise in patience and pain tolerance. Luc insisted that his leg didn't pain him nearly as much as it had the first few days, but Red could still see the pinch and strain on Luc's face as they worked to lower him into the water and to position his leg in as comfortable a way as possible. They were lucky Luc's knee hadn't been affected by the break, otherwise a bath would be impossible.

The result of manhandling Luc into the tub was that their bodies pressed and leaned against each other in a myriad of intimate ways, and they ended up tangled as Red supported most of Luc's weight. Red was soaked in seconds, in spite of remaining on the outside of the tub. But at long last, Luc was seated and able to recline against the towel draped across the back of the tub.

"I don't care that my leg is throbbing and that the water is lukewarm at best," Luc sighed. "This is the nicest I've felt in more than a week."

Red's instinct was to make exactly the sort of joke that Luc had made toward him just moments before, but he kept his mouth firmly shut.

Luc seemed to hear the implication anyhow. He glanced over his shoulder with a suggestive look, as if daring Red to say what he'd been thinking.

Instead, Red got up to fetch the washcloth and soap from the table and returned to hand them to Luc.

"I know you believe I am foolish to think that I don't deserve the high regard you've given me, but it is not a matter which you are free to have an opinion about," he said as he sat on a small stool beside the tub.

Luc flinched, his humor vanishing as he took the soap and washcloth from Red and began to scrub himself. "I beg to differ on that score. I would argue that your feelings and mine are intrinsically intertwined now."

Red shook his head. "My thoughts and my emotions, bastards though they are, are mine alone. Yes, I blame myself for the things I have done. I have committed great sins, and others have paid the price for them."

Luc shot him a sideways look of doubt. "Accidents—"

"Stop." Red held up a hand before Luc could pummel him with another platitude about how accidents happen and no one is at fault. "I feel guilty," he said, tapping his heart. "I hurt because of what I did, what happened because of my negligence. That is not going to change simply because you want it to or because Anthony wants it to, or because no one else blames me for it. I blame myself for it. I blame myself for surviving when others have died needlessly."

Luc's expression filled with compassion and his lips worked as though he would protest, but he never opened his mouth or said a word. His shoulders dropped a bit, and he stopped washing himself as he stared at the lip of the tub in front of him, at a loss.

Red sighed and reached into the water to take the cloth and soap from him. "My conscience will not let me rest easy, Luc," he said running the soap through the cloth until it was foamy, then handing the soap back to Luc. He gestured for Luc to lean forward so that he could scrub his back. "I know what you want from me," he went on in a quiet, almost morose voice, "but there is no space within me for that. I made a terrible mistake by attacking you the moment you arrived at Wodehouse Abbey. I thought I could fuck the pain away, but I fear I hurt you instead."

"You did not hurt me," Luc protested vehemently, twisting slightly to look over his shoulder at Red. He slumped slightly, then said, "Or perhaps I should say I was hurt, but I knew what I was in for, so I was complicit too. God, I was so randy and ready for you that I would have dragged you into the nearest cabinet and buggered you senseless if you hadn't jumped me first."

Red laughed in spite of himself, his face heating as he imagined it.

The trouble was, it was extraordinarily easy to imagine, particularly as he rubbed soap across the broad muscles of Luc's back. They always had been good together. Better than any of the other willing men he'd taken to his bed over the years. In spite of the laws of England and strictures of the Navy, bedfellows were easy to find. But Luc had always been different. They'd always enjoyed more than just each other's bodies. They sought out each other's company even when sex wasn't a possibility. Up until Shaw's death, Red had felt free to tell Luc anything, and he was eager to listen to any troubles Luc had in return.

There was a word for that, but it wasn't a word he was capable of facing. Not when other words, like "guilty", "careless", "destructive", and "failure" sat so heavily on his heart.

Those melancholy thoughts were superseded a moment later when Luc let out a long, impassioned moan. "That feels nice," he purred. "A little lower."

Heat rushed through Red all over again. He hadn't intended to bring Luc pleasure, it just seemed to happen when the two of them were together.

He did as requested, rubbing the soapy cloth down Luc's back, under the line of the water. Luc carried far more tension than he should have for a man in a bath, and Red did what he could to alleviate it. He let go of the cloth, pushing it around Luc's side in the water so that Luc could continue bathing whatever part of him needed it, then went to work kneading Luc's tight back.

The result was not only a loosening of tension in

Luc's muscles, desire pulsed through Red as fiercely as a storm. His blood raced through him and his heart thundered against his ribs. He used the excuse of kneading a particularly troublesome knot in Luc's back to lean in close to him, breathing in Luc's delicious scent, mixed with the rose of the soap.

When Luc let out a downright wicked moan, Red nearly unmanned himself in his breeches. He'd taken things too far, as usual, and now he was in trouble.

"Give me one moment," he said, his voice gruff with passion, standing abruptly and moving away from the tub. "I need to use the chamber pot."

He was already making a dash for the screen in the corner of the room as Luc said, "By all means," in a relaxed voice.

Cursing his intemperate body, Red reached for the fall of his breeches as soon as he was behind the screen and out of Luc's sight. Without ceremony, he freed his throbbing cock and took himself in hand. It took everything he had not to groan with pleasure as he stroked himself, leaning against the wall and closing his eyes. His imagination conjured up images of him and Luc in a bath together, soaping each other's bodies and devouring each other's mouths as he did. Within a minute, as he imagined how it might feel to impale himself on Luc's prick while the bathwater splashed and soaked the floor around them, he came across his hand.

It was impossible for him to completely swallow the grunt that came with his orgasm, but he prayed he had been quiet enough that Luc wouldn't know what he'd done. It was a blessing that his clothes were already soaked and that a small stack of rags rested on a table beside the chamber pot to assist with cleaning up. By the time he stepped back around the screen, his clothes were as much in order as they could be while splashed with bathwater, Red was convinced he would get away with his little adventure.

He was wrong.

Luc was already twisted in the tub, grinning at him the moment he stepped out from behind the screen. "Did you just step behind that screen to bring yourself off?"

"No!" Red lied immediately. It was pointless, though. His face was hotter than the sun, and no amount of avoiding Luc's gaze as he walked over to the table and pretended to be organizing its contents made him feel less guilty.

"Bloody hell, Red," Luc laughed. "If you needed a little relief, you should have let me bring you off."

Red's eyes went wide, and he abandoned fussing with the table to gape at Luc. "I would never do that."

"Why not?" Luc was still laughing at him. "Do you think I am any less randy than you right now?"

"I—" Red didn't have the first idea how to answer that.

"Because I am," Luc went on, arching one eyebrow mischievously, then lowering one hand under the water in front of him. "You've no idea how randy I've been for the last week, just the two of us alone in this room and me in nothing but a nightshirt the entire time." His face pinched with pleasure, and it was clear from the movements of his right arm what he was doing.

"Stop that at once," Red said, stepping away from the table and closer to the tub.

That was the wrong thing to do. For one, Luc did not stop. For another, Red's new position gave him a clear view of the work of Luc's hand under the water. Luc's prick was hard and thick, and its tip flared as he stroked himself. The whole thing had a dreamlike quality as the ripples in the water distorted everything Red was seeing.

"You're going to injure yourself further," Red warned him, heat and prickles of renewed desire shooting down his spine.

"It feels so delicious, Red." Luc tipped his head back, eyes closed, groaning as he increased his speed and intensity. "Almost as good as when your mouth is around me, swallowing me deep, and your tongue—" He cut himself off with a groan.

"Luc, I'm warning you," Red told him, his own voice thick with lust.

"What are you going to do?" Luc panted, opening his eyes and staring right at Red like the very devil as he stroked. "Are you going to spank me for being bad?"

"You bastard," Red growled at him—though he teetered on the edge of mad laughter as he did. Especially when Luc let out a cry and spurted ribbons of pearly essence into the water as he spoke.

Red's whole body clenched with desire as he watched Luc tighten, then relax once he'd milked every last drop. He flopped against the edge of the tub with such blissful contentment that Red couldn't help but let his lips quirk into a grin. Apparently, Luc was right—a broken leg meant nothing when it came to the functioning of a man's cock.

"Are you quite pleased with yourself?" he asked in a scolding tone all the same, crossing his arms and staring down at Luc like the disobedient brat he was.

"So very, very pleased," Luc purred, opening one eye only to peek up at Red.

Red shook his head, his heart feeling lighter than it had in a very long time. "You'd better let me help you out of that tub before you end up with spunk soaking your bandage. That would ruin the entire purpose of the bath."

"Come on, then," Luc laughed, adjusting himself to be ready for Red to help hoist him to his feet.

Red moved to stand behind him, reaching his arms under Luc's and heaving. Once again, concentrating on the physical task at hand distracted them both from the teasing and the tension between them. It was even more of a task to maneuver Luc out of the tub, then for Red to dry him before they could walk back to the bed and see to the splint and bandage.

In spite of the wickedness of what they'd each done, Red was glad he'd relieved himself before rubbing towels all over Luc's body, or clasping Luc's naked body close to his as they struggled back to the bed. Injury or no injury, Red wasn't certain what he would have done if he'd still been aroused to the point of insensibility with Luc so dependent on him.

Red took so much care removing the wet bandages on Luc's leg and peeling away the soaked splints that it was almost comical.

"My leg is not made of glass," Luc scolded him, though his movements were ginger as he patted his leg dry.

"Perhaps not," Red said as he dashed to the table to fetch the clean, dry bandages and replacement splints Dr. Norris had left, "but it is still broken."

"You can already tell it's healing," Luc insisted, leaning back and staring at his two, stretched legs in front of him as Red brought the things back to the bed.

Red glanced at Luc's legs with a more skeptical eye. The huge bruise that had enveloped the site of the break had faded into ugly colors. The ridge of

Luc's shin bone was visible beneath the skin, now that the swelling had gone down. It was no longer a straight, clean line, like his left shin. There was a distinct jaggedness where the bone should have been smooth. More noticeable still, at least to Red at the angle where he stood, was the fact that Luc's right leg was very subtly shorter than his left now. It might not have been a break clean through the bone, but enough damage had been done that the effects would be permanent.

Red swallowed and went to work fastening a new splint and bandages the way Dr. Norris had shown him. He tried not to let his hands shake as he worked, and he did his best to wind the bandage as tightly as he could without cutting off circulation to Luc's foot.

"Red," Luc spoke softly when Red was almost done. When Red glanced up at him, Luc smiled softly and said, "It's alright. You may not be willing to hear it yet, but I will say it regardless. I forgive you for this. I forgive you for everything, and I always will. It would be impossible for me not to."

Red's throat squeezed tight at the words he didn't feel he deserved. For once, he wouldn't argue with Luc that he didn't deserve them. Just as he had attempted to explain that his guilt was his to foster without interference from anyone else, so Luc's forgiveness was his to give as freely as he wanted it.

He nodded, then focused on his work. "Let's get this sorted, and I'll call Daniel and Robbie to carry you downstairs while I put on something more suitable for company."

"You aren't going to join the others looking like that?" Luc teased him. "I find you rather fetching in nothing but a soaked shirt and breeches, which, by the way, you have fastened incorrectly." He winked, filling Red with warmth like the first rays of sunlight breaking through the last frost of winter.

Red glanced quickly down, only to find that his breeches were in perfect order. "You bastard," he said, shaking his head and almost laughing. The moment was so close to the way things had been between the two of them before that it took Red's breath away. He hid his emotion by saying, "Percy would just love it if I paraded in front of him in a state of undress." He moved to fetch Luc's clothes—including a pair of breeches that had been specially modified to accommodate the splint.

The simple task felt far more important than it should. Something had changed between him and Luc, that much was certain. What it was and how Red might embrace it were different matters entirely, though. As pleasant as the time the two of them had spent together was, Red worried that it was merely the calm at the eye of the hurricane.

14

There was hope. No matter what else might happen, no matter how difficult it would be for Luc to resume some sort of ordinary occupation once his leg was healed, there was hope that things between him and Red might return to the way they had been before. No, there was a chance that they could be even better than that. There was a chance that Luc might be able to forge the kind of life he wanted, with Red by his side, no matter which way the other winds of his life and career blew.

But the entire situation was still tenuous at best.

"Are you certain this is advisable?" Clarence asked, his voice overly loud as usual, as Daniel and Robbie, the footmen, hefted Luc off of the same detached door they'd used to transport him the day he'd been injured onto the settee in the conservatory.

As it was a gloomy, overcast day, most of the Abbey's guests were gathered in the conservatory for games, reading, and conversation. Septimus was apparently up in the nursery, assisting Mr. Seymour in teaching a history lesson to Lord Francis and Lady Eliza—who had recovered from their brief illnesses—

and Spencer was nowhere to be found either, but the rest of them, including Mr. Haight, were there.

"Dr. Norris agreed that I could be brought down for a bit of company as long as I remained stationary and took great care of my leg," Luc told Clarence with a broad smile. "I, for one, am devilishly glad to see something other than the four walls of my bedchamber, and to keep company with the lot of you together.

"And where is your faithful nursemaid?" Barrett asked with a knowing grin as he moved one of the chairs closer to the settee so that he could talk with Luc. More likely, he wanted to keep a protective eye on him to ensure he didn't jostle his leg.

Luc smirked at Barrett and said, "Red was in need of a change of clothes after assisting me with my bath this morning."

Barrett barked out a laugh. "I'd wager he was."

He looked as though he would say more—likely something ribald and entirely inappropriate—but Mr. Haight glanced up from where he was playing cards with Anthony at a small table close to the pianoforte, which Lord Sigglesthorpe was playing with gusto.

As soon as Barrett realized he'd been heard, he snapped his mouth shut, cleared his throat, and shared a relieved look with Luc the moment Haight turned back to his cards. "It's been lovely seeing Red care for you this last week," he said in far more measured tones.

"The two of us have been dear friends these many years now," Luc said with a smile, praying he spoke carefully enough that Mr. Haight wouldn't read more into the conversation. "Though I wish he weren't caring for me so much out of guilt."

Barrett shrugged and leaned back into his chair.

"Red deserves a little guilt after the way he lost his temper."

Luc's own temper flared so fast at that statement that the corresponding jerk sent a brief burst of pain through his leg. "Redmond has been through quite a bit in the last few months and you know it. His soul is unsettled, and he needs time to be at peace with himself again."

Surprisingly, Mr. Haight glanced up from his card game once more, but this time with more emotion than Luc would have expected after such a simple comment. More than that, the older man's expression tightened with sympathy in such a way that Luc was left wondering what sort of sins and pains he had experienced in his own life. Of course, a man who had made his fortune in industry might very well have a great deal to regret, if the things Luc had heard about conditions in those sorts of factories and mills were to be believed.

What surprised Luc even more were the cagey looks that Barrett and Anthony wore, and even the way Clarence seemed to find a pile of sheet music on one of the shelves at the far side of the room extraordinarily interesting.

"Redmond will come around," he said at last, feeling rather like he was the only one who hadn't heard the punchline of the latest joke making the rounds. "I believe that a good deal of his restlessness comes from not knowing what to do with himself, now that the war is over."

Another set of cautious, anxious looks flew around the room.

"Do you know what you plan to do with yourself now?" Barrett asked quietly.

Luc's chest tightened. He had purposely shoved all

of those thoughts aside, pouring his energy and emotions into the riddle that was Red and his bruised soul. He'd seen the truth right in front of him that morning, before Red had reassembled his splint and bandage. The length of his right leg had been changed. It was barely noticeable, and perhaps with a slightly thicker sole in his shoes going forward he would be able to walk, perhaps even run, without any visible impairment. But the Admiralty wasn't likely to see things with as much leniency.

All the same, Luc smiled at Barrett and said, "I am endeavoring to think no farther than the day in front of me until I am able to cast off this splint and amble around your family's property once more."

Barrett sent him a sidelong look that said he wasn't fooled, and that he knew as well as Luc that the broken leg changed everything.

Red strode into the room before the conversation could go any further, though.

"Who is this strange man?" Clarence teased him, stepping away from the shelf and rejoining the conversation. "I recall someone I once knew who resembled him somewhat, but it has been ages since I've seen that fellow."

"Bugger off, Clarence," Red said with a grin. He immediately lost his smugness when he spotted Mr. Haight playing cards with Anthony. "That is...er...I did not mean...."

"This is not the first time I have ever spent the morning in the company of other men," Mr. Haight laughed. "And do not let my age and upright appearance fool you. I began life as a shipwright's son in Blackwall. I've heard far worse."

That seemed to appease Red, and it made Clarence laugh out loud. "How did a shipwright's son end up as a wealthy factory owner, then?" Clarence asked, striding across the room to take a seat at the table with Mr. Haight and Anthony while Red moved to perch on the very end of the settee with Luc, keeping his distance.

"Through hard work, perseverance, and devilishly good luck," Haight answered.

"And what brought you to iron manufacturing instead of opening a cotton mill or some other sort of factory?" Clarence asked on, leaning back in his chair.

"The war," Haight said with a simple shrug before playing one of his cards. "The demand for iron to aid with the production of weaponry and such for battle made my fortune."

"You profited off of the deaths of all those men?" Red asked.

Luc could see his temper rising—and a great deal of anguish with it—so he tapped him with his good foot and frowned in warning.

"No, Lord Beverley," Haight said with a kind smile for Red. "I profited because I owned powerful blast furnaces that could produce a raw material that was used for a great many things. Arms manufacturers who supplied the British Army and Navy were only some of my customers. In fact, the single largest customer I had during the war—and the one who continues to keep my business afloat, now that demand due to the war has fallen off drastically—is a company that manufactures nails."

"Nails?" Clarence repeated, his brow shooting up.

"I would imagine that there is a high demand for nails at the moment," Anthony added, playing one of his cards as well. "What with all of the new construction taking place, both at home and abroad."

"You would be astounded to know how much of

the trade I do is with the very countries who were our enemies just a few short years ago," Haight went on, laying down another card. "The simple fact of the matter is that England is years, perhaps decades, ahead of the rest of Europe when it comes to the advances of industry, and since we can offer more of a product at a cheaper price than anyone else, even our recent enemies have become our most reliable customers."

"Because everyone needs nails," Luc said, his mind spinning as he contemplated the implications.

"What about these new steam engines that so many people are so mad about?" Sigglesthorpe asked, pounding the last notes of the song he'd been playing, then leaving the pianoforte. He gravitated to Luc's side instead of joining the group at the table. "I have been given to understand that steam engines are on the rise, and they require iron, do they not?" He addressed his question to Luc, for some reason, and the way he emphasized certain words made the entire thing sound salacious instead of practical.

"They do," Haight answered from the table, his gaze focused on his card. "And I agree with those men who you say are mad about steam engines. I believe we are only beginning to tap their potential."

"Yes, and they have so very much potential to tap," Sigglesthorpe said, wiggling his eyebrows at Luc.

Luc's mouth pulled into a grin, and it was all he could do not to laugh, particularly when he saw the startled look on Red's face. Luc knew when he was being flirted with, and Lord Sigglesthorpe was most definitely flirting. Luc could only guess that the man was doing it purposely to antagonize Red, since he and Red had been friends from childhood. Or else

Sigglesthorpe truly was as much of a coquette as he pretended to be.

"Is that what sort of a factory you wish to build here, on the property of Wodehouse Abbey?" Clarence asked, his face pinched with distaste. "Aren't they dreadfully dirty?"

"Dreadfully dirty," Sigglesthorpe repeated as he leaned against the head of the settee, his hips at the level of Luc's eyes. "Just as I like things."

Luc had to clamp a hand to his mouth to keep from barking a laugh. As it was, he snorted enough to fall into a coughing fit. That sent stabs of pain through his leg, which sobered both him and Sigglesthorpe up a bit. "Are you trying to finish the job Red started, my lord?" Luc murmured to Sigglesthorpe quietly enough that the group at the table wouldn't hear him.

"I have been told I am adept at finishing men off," Sigglesthorpe whispered in return.

"Cheeky," Luc giggled in return.

"Dead," Red muttered, glaring at Sigglesthorpe.

Sigglesthorpe was utterly unrepentant. "One man's cast-offs are another man's treasure," he told Red, batting his eyes and sliding his hand across the back of the settee, close enough that he could have threaded his fingers in Luc's hair if he wanted to.

Luc nearly burst into another fit of coughing laughter. He suddenly wondered how much he and Red and their tangled relationship had been discussed among the other guests of Wodehouse Abbey during his convalescence. He might have only known Sigglesthorpe a short time, but it was entirely likely the man was attempting to light a fire under Red's arse, goading him into making a move that would ensure his happiness by behaving as though he would claim Luc in his stead.

"...which is why I plan to branch out into more commercial types of production," Haight had continued at the table, evidently outlining exactly what his plans for a Wodehouse Abbey factory were. "The area is unsuitable for iron manufacture, but with a port like Hull so close, it could be ideal for a smaller factory that produces household goods of some sort."

"I still have a difficult time imagining smoke belched from factory furnaces covering this beautiful land," Clarence said with a shake of his head. He, at least, was still engaged in the conversation with Haight.

"Not all factories need to operate in such a manner," Haight said with a shrug. "Some can be very modest indeed. Though all machinery of production is better run with steam power."

"I have yet to decide whether I wish to carve up my ancestral home, even for a manufacturing endeavor that produces domestic goods," Anthony said, as though he were reassuring Clarence. He followed that by setting down the remainder of his cards and saying, "I believe that is a clear victory for me, sir."

Haight set down the last of his cards with a laugh. "I have half a mind to believe you and your friends distracted me with all this talk of factories simply so that you could win the game, Your Grace."

"I would never do such a thing," Anthony replied with a wink.

"I would," Sigglesthorpe added for Luc and Red—and Barrett, who was still seated beside the settee and seemed content to watch everyone's interactions as though he were attending the theater. "I always play to win," he added, leaning close to Luc's ear and staring saucily at Red as he did.

"You've made your point, Percy," Red growled, eyes narrowed.

"Yes, I believe I have." Sigglesthorpe straightened and moved away from Luc with an expression that all but confirmed he was flirting with Luc to prompt action from Red. Sigglesthorpe sent Luc a final, conspiratorial look as he made his way back to the pianoforte, then sat and played the opening strains of a sentimental love song.

"The Wodehouse family has quite a colorful variety of friends," Luc commented casually to Barrett, grinning widely.

"Yes, they do indeed," Barrett replied with a wink.

"I would tell the two of you to sod off, but you would probably take it as a suggestion," Red grumbled. He pushed himself up off the settee and stalked to the other side of the room, where tea was laid out.

"Red's spirits are much improved," Barrett commented, leaning closer to Luc. "It has me wondering who is healing who."

"I would like to think it's a bit of both," Luc said with a smile, watching as Red poured not one, but two cups of tea. His affectionate smile dropped to a troubled frown, though. "I just wish he didn't still have such a long way to go," he sighed, then pried his eyes away to glance at Barrett with more sentimentality than he intended. "He refuses to love me, and the longer he holds out against what we both know is inevitable, the more I fear he'll walk away from us for good," he said in the softest of whispers, careful not to be overheard by Haight.

"He never would," Barrett insisted, shaking his head. "He spoke of nothing but you for weeks before you arrived here, and before, during the war, he lived for the moments the two of you could find together.

He can fight it all he'd like, but you are the safe harbor he will eventually drop anchor in."

Luc snorted with laughter, even as Red glanced over his shoulder to see what he and Barrett were laughing about. As Red started back in their direction with two cups of tea, Luc quickly said, "I don't know if that is the loveliest thing anyone has ever said to me or the rudest. Though I wouldn't mind one bit if that salty sailor would drop anchor in my harbor right now," he added with a touch of wistfulness.

It was Barrett's turn to swallow a laugh. "Feeling a bit stuck in a calm, are we?" he teased. "Is your deck in need of a good swabbing?"

"I could stand to have some of the barnacles scraped off, yes," Luc chuckled in return.

Red eyed them both warily when he returned to the settee and handed Luc one of the cups of tea. "I am well aware the two of you are gossiping about me."

"Of course we are," Barrett said, getting up, then slapping Red on the shoulder before gesturing for him to take his seat. "You haven't been downstairs in days, for which you deserve as much teasing as possible."

Barrett headed across the room to join what looked like a game of whist that Anthony, Clarence, and Haight were beginning.

Red sat in the vacated chair and sipped his tea sullenly.

Luc shook his head. "Are you upset because you've friends who care enough about you to poke fun at you, or are you more jealous that your friend, Lord Sigglesthorpe, was flirting with me to make you jealous."

"I am not jealous of Percy," Red grumbled, sinking into the chair. "You would never concern yourself with him anyhow."

"Wouldn't I?" Luc lifted his brow, feigning an interest in Sigglesthorpe as he played an extra flourish at the end of the verse of his song. "The man is clearly good with his hands, and since I have been sorely lacking in relief through this last week, I should ask him to use them."

Red nearly choked on his tea. When he recovered, he glared at Luc. "Alright, your point is taken. You want me, and you want me to stop dithering."

"Bloody right you are," Luc said with a nod before drinking a bit of his tea. He didn't want to leave it there, though, so he gathered all of his courage and laid his heart on the line. "So why not share the bed with me tonight instead of monitoring me from a chair across the room, like some aged nanny keeping watch over her charge?"

Red swallowed his mouthful of tea awkwardly, then coughed to clear his throat. "You want me to share a bed with you?"

Luc's heart suddenly caught in his throat. Red had inadvertently given him an opening to discuss the one thing he wanted to talk to Red openly about, but had been too anxious, or injured, to address directly. He wanted the two of them to stop pretending the ties that bound them together were just for fun. He wanted Red to throw his lot in with him forever, no matter what that life together might look like.

But there were others in the room, and as softly as they might speak, a conversation as important as the one they needed to have must be a private one.

"You've done it before," Luc said instead, shrugging. "The bed has to be a damn sight more comfortable than the chair you've spent the last week attempting to sleep in."

"I've retired to my own room when I knew you

were asleep, so it hasn't been as bad as all that," Red defended himself.

Luc arched one eyebrow at him, reasonably certain Red was lying to spare his feelings. "Whatever will I do if I need someone to help me *use the chamber pot* in the middle of the night?"

Red's face turned bright scarlet, and they both knew exactly why.

Which was why Luc was shocked when Red mumbled, "Very well, then. I will stay with you through the night and sleep in your bed. But if I kick out and break your leg all over again, this time, the fault will be yours."

Luc chuckled at the morose way Red spoke and finished his tea. Deep in his heart, he couldn't have been happier. The two of them were making progress. Luc was beginning to feel as though they might find their safe harbor after all.

15

R ed had no idea what had possessed him to agree to Luc's mad plan for him to sleep in the bed that night. He'd done perfectly fine on the chair in the corner for the last week. It might have meant a long week of precious little sleep, sore muscles, and bones that were likely never to recover from the awkward angles and odd shapes they'd been jarred into, but it had meant he'd been close to Luc. But not too close.

Sleeping fitfully in a chair for a week had had an entirely unexpected effect as well. Red hadn't once been plagued by his nightmares of Shaw's death in all that time. It was a relief in so many ways. Between the solace of not dreaming at all for the entire length of Luc's recovery so far and the joy of being close to Luc —a joy he still didn't believe he deserved—Red let his guard down.

"I refuse to sleep tucked up against you," Red informed Luc late that night as they went through their preparations for sleep. "If you were hoping for a bit of a cuddle, you will continue hoping in vain."

Luc laughed—likely at Red's dour tone—as the

two of them worked together to settle him on his back on the right-hand side of the bed. Red had already helped Luc to a quick sponge bath, which had renewed both of their ardor and left them far more energetic than they should have been while preparing for a long night's sleep.

"Are you certain you don't need to *use the chamber pot* before climbing in with me, then?" Luc teased. "Since there won't be any *cuddling*?"

Red pursed his lips and frowned at Luc as he jerked the bedcovers up and tucked them tightly around his neck, hiding his entire body. "I knew allowing you downstairs was a terrible idea," he groused. "Percy has had too much of an influence on you, and now you're as difficult as a march hare to manage."

Luc continued to chuckle as Red stepped away from the bed to finish his own ablutions. "Nothing has warmed my heart more or made me feel so jolly as watching you turn green with envy as Lord Sigglesthorpe flirted with me today."

Red scowled and glanced over his shoulder at Luc. He removed his toothbrush from his mouth and replied with a frothy, "Do not read too much into it. Percy flirts with anything that had a cock he can suck."

That only made Luc laugh harder, which most certainly had not been Red's intention.

"You are deliciously jealous." Luc positioned his arms behind his head and watched as Red finished with his teeth, rinsed and spat, ran a washcloth over his face, then set to work carefully arranging the jar of tooth powder, the soap, both his and Luc's razors, and everything they would need in the morning. "Honestly, Red, you have nothing to be concerned about," Luc went on as Red finally dragged himself over to the left side of the bed. "Sigglesthorpe is pretty, but he isn't you."

Red's heart caught in his chest at the sudden sentimentality of Luc's words. Luc had confessed his love, and even if he hadn't, Red would have known it was there. But something about the domesticity of climbing into bed with Luc, dressed in his nightshirt with a hole under one arm, after Luc had watched him brush his teeth, felt far more momentous than any flowery declarations of undying passion whispered under a stary sky or in a garden filled with roses.

"Good night, Luc," Red said, his voice hoarse with the sudden anxiety of it all.

"Don't I get a goodnight kiss?" Luc teased him.

"No," Red grumbled, turning to his side so his back was to Luc.

Luc continued to laugh at him, reaching out a hand to touch Red's back.

That single touch was like fire. It was one thing to hear Luc say "I love you," but words could be brushed off and forgotten. That light touch, the tenderness and implication of the two of them in bed together, and the easy manner the two of them had with each other —like they were a matched pair of gloves—was far more difficult to ignore.

It took more than an hour for Red to fall asleep as the confusion of everything that was and could be between him and Luc whirled through his mind. Luc's breathing steadied into slumber fairly quickly, but Red resisted sleep. He was careful not to move lest he accidentally kick Luc's leg. He'd purposely chosen to sleep on Luc's left side to stay as far away from his injured leg as possible.

Red's worry went deeper than that, though. He'd

already broken Luc's body. If the two of them stayed close, if he accepted Luc's idea that he was in love as serious and lasting, how long would it be before he injured Luc's heart or his spirit? He seemed to ruin everything and everyone wherever he went. What was stopping him from hurting Luc in a much more grievous way?

At last, sleep claimed him, but it was not the relief he'd hoped for.

THE SUN BEAT down merrily on the deck of the Majesty. Red strode from the fore to the aft, his hands behind his back, surveying the work of the Majesty's crew. The mood of the ship was tranquil, merry. A group of the Majesty's sailors sang shanties and danced the hornpipe while others worked. Red let them play, let his men enjoy themselves, now that the war was over. It was his watch, after all, which meant he made the rules and was responsible for everyone's actions.

His watch. He was responsible. Everything that happened on his watch was his responsibility.

Storm clouds moved in fast from the horizon in every direction, as if the Majesty were the center of the universe. Sea birds cried out and circled overhead, as if they knew something horrible was about to happen. Red continued to smile, oblivious to the trouble that was about to hit him and change his life forever. Red watched it all, watched himself, as though he were standing outside of a painting gazing in.

"What-ho, Billy!" a voice shouted from high overhead in the rigging. "Watch this!"

Red glanced up. He knew what he would see, knew what would happen next.

But instead of Oliver Shaw climbing around the rigging, like the monkey Red had accused him of being, Luc was the one scampering across the yardarm. He grabbed hold of a rope that hung loose from the fore topsail yard. With one of his exuberant laughs, Luc pushed off of the yard and flew through the air in a wide arc. He sailed like one of the seagulls circling around him.

And then the rope broke. Smile still on his face, Luc plummeted to the deck.

"No!" Red shouted, racing forward. As hard as he ran and as desperately as he reached out, some invisible force held him back.

Luc fell fast, but through what felt like an impossible distance. His lively smile transformed slowly into the grimace of pain that he'd worn immediately after his leg was broken. Still he fell, and still Red tried to fight through whatever had him in its grip to reach Luc in time to catch him. But instead of moving forward, Luc was somehow growing farther and farther away from him, as if a hook had lodged in his stomach and was yanking him backward, into an abyss.

At last, Luc hit the ship's deck and shattered into a million pieces. His body disappeared entirely, bursting into a cloud of glittering, red shards. The blast spread fast, like the impact of a cannonball, covering everything in its path in blood and stealing the air from Red's lungs.

RED JOLTED awake with a stifled cry. He sat up abruptly, gasping for breath and covered in sweat. The dream had felt so real to him, as it always did. He could still smell the salt of the sea. His skin still prickled from where the glittering shards of Luc had pierced him like a thousand tiny needles. The horror of everything he'd seen washed over him, and no matter how many times he tried to tell himself it was just a dream, he couldn't shake the fear it'd left him with.

The one blessing was that Luc continued to sleep peacefully on his side of the bed. By some miracle, Red hadn't disturbed him at all.

As delicately as he could, Red slipped out of bed. As soon as his bare feet hit the floor, he paused to still his breathing. He was awake, alive, part of the real world. Luc hadn't fallen to his death. He was right there, in bed, undisturbed.

Red was determined to keep him that way. He tip-toed across the room to where he'd left his banyan, snatched the garment up and threw it over his shoulders, then hurried out of the room. He tied the banyan with shaking hands as he reached the hall, but as he approached the door to his own bedchamber, he changed his mind about hiding away for the rest of the night and made for the stairs instead. Anthony kept brandy and port in his study, and more than anything, in that moment, Red needed a drink.

"Oh! I beg your pardon!"

The moment Red turned the corner into the study, he was surprised to find Haight ensconced in one of the wide chairs, a book in one hand and a glass of port in the other, looking equally as startled as Red felt.

"Mr. Haight." Red hesitated in the doorway. "I did not realize you were awake."

"I thought I was the only one," Haight replied with a guilty, yet somehow still charming, look. "I could not sleep," he went on, relaxing into a smile and closing his book. "Too many important thoughts rattling around my brain."

"Yes," Red said slowly, advancing into the room. "Me as well." It was a bit of a lie, but he didn't think Haight would fault him for it. He headed to the cabinet where the port was kept and helped himself to a glass.

"Were you perhaps worried over your friend, Mr. Salterford?" Haight asked with a gently inquisitive arch of one eyebrow.

A sizzle of wariness shot down Red's spine. Had Haight figured out what was between him and Luc? Had he figured out Anthony and Barrett's connection? Or Septimus and Seymour's for that matter?

As soon as those thoughts struck him, Red pushed them aside. If Haight had puzzled it all out, he wouldn't still be there. Either he didn't know or he did and it was of no consequence to him.

"It is a difficult thing, when one causes such grievous bodily harm to one's friend," he said at last, taking his port and moving to sit in the chair opposite Haight.

Haight hummed and nodded sadly. He set his book aside completely, then took a sip of his port. "I have felt that burden of conscience before," he admitted.

Red's brow shot up. He took a large drink of port before asking, "You have?"

Haight smiled sadly and focused his gaze on Red instead of the empty fireplace. "I own factories, Lord Beverley. As careful as I have tried to be in the pursuit of industry and profit, men have died on premises that belong to me, crushed or maimed by machinery that I own. Some men may not let such things attack their consciences, but I do."

Red shifted uncomfortably in his chair, uncertain

how he felt about the confession. "Do you know how many men have died in your factories?" he asked, immediately feeling as though he shouldn't have and covering the awkwardness by taking another long drink.

"Fourteen," Haight answered without hesitation. "I could tell you their names as well, if you have any interest in that."

Red shook his head, his throat constricting. He studied Haight, looking for some sign that the man was a murderer, that he was the very devil himself. All he saw was a tired man with grey hair with most of his life already behind him. He saw a kind man, a man who took care to learn the names of the men who had lost their lives for him. None of it fit with what he thought he should be feeling.

"How do you face those deaths and continue to live?" he asked in a hushed voice, his heart pounding against his ribs.

Haight shrugged. "Sometimes it is difficult. I ask myself if all this industrial advancement is worth the lives that have been lost. Is the faster, easier production of goods worth the loss of a single life in the bowels of the machinery that make it possible? Is the illness that results from conditions in cotton mills throughout England a fair price to pay for the advancement of all mankind?" He shrugged again, this time with a deeper sadness in his eyes.

"You cannot stop industry from advancing, though," Red said. He liked Haight and was seized with a deep need to reassure the man. "If not you, then someone far less scrupulous will come along and exploit the laborers that are necessary to lift all mankind into a new era of industry."

Haight smiled slightly. "Are you saying that the

deaths and disfigurements would have happened any-how, whether I owned the factory or not?"

Red blinked, then answered, "Yes. Not only that, but the demand for the goods that are produced from your factory's iron would still be there. And with that demand, the need for workers to operate the ma-chinery would still exist. I take it your factory is not manned by slave labor."

"It is not," Haight said with a nod. He had a grand-fatherly smile in his eyes that seemed especially pointed as he watched Red. "One could argue that the workers in my factories took employment there of their own volition." He took a gulp of his port, then went on with, "One could argue that economic neces-sity drove them to take employment they would not have chosen otherwise."

"There is always a choice," Red argued.

"There is," Haight agreed. His expression grew even more focused on Red, sending curiosity burning through him. He looked like he wanted to say some-thing but was holding back.

Red narrowed his eyes slightly. "I feel as though you have further advice for me, but I cannot for the life of me make out what it might be."

Haight let out a breath and tipped his glass up, draining it, then setting it aside. "Your brother begged me not to tell you."

Red's curiosity burned hotter than ever. "Tell me what?"

Haight was silent for a long moment before asking a question Red did not expect. "Do you think that young lads who join the Navy in search of ad-venture do so voluntarily or because they are forced?"

Wary prickles raced down Red's back, and he wondered if he was back in his nightmare. "I do not know," he said in a hollow voice.

"I do know," Haight said with a sad smile. "My grandson wanted nothing more than to join the Navy and go off to sea from the time he was old enough to speak. He loved watching the ships sail up and down the Thames. He was always there when cargo from my factories was loaded onto one sailing vessel or another. He knew the name of every ship that came into port, and he could tell you where they had been and how long their journeys were. None of us could have kept him from the sea if we'd tried."

Desperate panic clawed at Red's insides, and his eyes stung with the memory of Oliver Shaw's bright laughter and enthusiasm in all things.

"I was able to purchase him a position as a midshipman, thanks to my good fortune," Haight went on. "And I believe that is how you met Oliver, Lord Beverley."

Red burst into tears at the revelation. "I'm sorry," he said setting his port aside, sliding out of his chair, and dropping to his knees, head bent toward Haight. "I am so sorry. It was all my fault. I never should have let them play in the rigging like that."

"Shh, shh." Haight soothed him by placing a hand on Red's head and stroking his hair. "It wasn't your fault, Lord Beverley. Everyone from your Captain Wallace to Oliver's friend Billy has told me as much. Wallace wrote to my daughter, Oliver's mother, telling her in no uncertain terms that Oliver was loved and cared for by all of the officers of the *Majesty*. He insisted that Oliver was one of the happiest young men he'd ever known, and that it was simply an accident and a tragedy that his life was ended too soon."

"I should have stopped him," Red continued to

wail, resting his forehead on Haight's knees. "It was my watch, my responsibility. They weren't supposed to be playing."

"Was it my responsibility when George Bednar was dragged into the smelting machine and killed in my factory because he was making a spectacle of himself in front of his friends?" Haight asked. "Was it the foreman on duty's fault?"

Red wanted to answer no, but he wasn't ready to shrug the burden of guilt from his shoulders yet.

"Accidents happen, Lord Beverley," Haight went on in a soft voice, still smoothing Red's hair as his shoulders heaved with sobs. "We can try as we might, but we cannot hold back the hands of Fate. God has His purpose for us all, and whether it seems cruel to us in the moment or not, He has designs for all of us."

"I want nothing to do with a god who would hurl a lad of fourteen to his death before he had a chance to live," Red groaned, glancing up at Haight, his face stained with tears.

"Oh, so it is God's fault that our Oliver is with Him now?" Haight asked with an impossible grin, though his eyes were filled with tears as well.

Red flopped his head to rest on Haight's knees again. "I could have done better," he whispered. "I should have prevented it."

"Would you say that of another officer, your friend, Lord Copeland, for example, had he been the one taking that watch?" Haight asked.

The answer was an instant "No." Red would never have blamed Barrett if it had been his watch.

Haight's hand stilled on his head. "I have other reasons that I should apologize to you, Lord Beverley," he said.

Red glanced up, baffled. "You? Apologize to me?"

Haight smiled sadly, then said, "I knew full well that you and some of the other officers from Oliver's ship were in residence here before I came. I would not have considered the property of Wodehouse Abbey for a factory at all, but your names were mentioned in connection with the land. I came here because I wished to talk with you all about Oliver. Consider it an old man's sentimentality, but I wanted to recapture a bit of my grandson."

"But...but why did you not tell anyone?" Red asked, kneeling straighter.

It hit him a moment later when Haight smiled sadly.

"You did tell them," he said, sucking in a breath. "They all know. The rest of them knew from the start."

"They do, and they did," Haight confessed. "You and your friend, Mr. Salterford, were out walking when I revealed the purpose of my visit. However, your brother and the other officers urged me to keep the truth from you. They informed me that you were racked with guilt over Oliver's death and that you needed time before you were ready to speak with me about it."

Red's mouth dropped open, but he didn't know what to say. Anthony and the others had been right. Part of him wanted to be angry with them, but he couldn't be. They had gone out of their way to protect him.

"The secret is out now," Haight said, resting his hand on Red's hot cheek as though Red were the grandson he had lost. "Have I disturbed you too much by telling you?"

Red paused to think, then shook his head. "I was already disturbed."

"My poor boy," Haight sighed. Red wasn't certain

whether he meant Oliver or him. "Please do not blame yourself for the turning of the wheel of fate," he went on. "It was Oliver's time, even if that seems wrong and insensible to us. The best way to honor my grandson's memory, to honor the memories of all those who gave their lives in service to king and country, is not to cease to live your life, but to live it to the fullest. I dare say that you knew my grandson better than I did in those last years of his life. How would Oliver have wanted you to live for him? What stories will he want you to tell him when the two of you are inevitably re-united in God's kingdom?"

Red's throat and chest squeezed and tears came to his eyes all over again at the heady thought. "I don't know," he whispered hoarsely.

"Perhaps you should give it some thought," Haight said with a wink. He pulled his hand back, then pushed himself to stand. Red got up quickly and moved out of his way. "Now, if you will excuse me, I suddenly feel as though the weight that has been hovering over me, preventing me from sleeping, has lifted. I am more than ready to tuck myself away in your brother's most excellent guestroom and to dream away the rest of the night. I suggest you do the same, my lord."

Haight nodded respectfully to Red, patted his shoulder one last time, then strode out of the room.

Red watched him go, his heart racing. He wasn't certain how he felt, other than that he felt as though his soul had been strapped to the mainmast and forced to withstand a hurricane. Forgiveness felt as though it hung in the air in front of him, but his arms were still tied, preventing him from grasping it.

He needed more time to think. More than anything, he wanted to talk to Luc about it all. But Luc was sleeping peacefully, and Red didn't dare disturb him. The only other option was to tell his troubles to the moonlight and to the sea.

Still in his banyan and nightshirt, he left the study and sought a door that would take him out of the house so that he could walk down to the beach and hopefully into the arms of forgiveness.

16

L uc would not be sorry when his leg was finally healed and his splint and bandage were gone. Sleeping wasn't impossible with his leg held forcibly immobile, but he would have much preferred to sleep on his side than his back.

Truth be told, he would much rather sleep on his side while resting against Red, who actually did prefer sleeping on his back, for some ungodly reason. It was yet another reason why the two of them fit so well together, both physically and in terms of their dispositions. They were like two halves of a shell that protected a precious pearl of love and friendship between them.

Luc laughed quietly as his mind conjured up that image in the hazy space between sleep and wakefulness. Leaving the Navy had turned him into a sentimental fool. Or perhaps extended proximity to Red had done that to him. They'd never spent so much time in such close quarters while serving aboard two different ships. Even if those ships were sisters who had prowled the waters of Canada together. Luc had been anxious that so much time together would be too much for him and Red, but as far as he was concerned, it was exactly the opposite. The more time Luc spent with Red, the more he wanted to spend.

He reached out to his left, intent on telling Red as much, whether the man's guilt would let him listen or not, and his hand hit nothing but an empty sheet beside him.

He opened his eyes and sucked in a breath, turning his head to find that Red wasn't there with him. A twist of fear squeezed his heart, but Luc ignored it.

"Red?" he called out, his voice still hazy from sleep. "Don't tell me you needed to use the chamber pot already." If it came down to it, Luc was certain the two of them could find any number of ways to bugger each other silly that wouldn't jostle or further injure his leg.

The room was silent in response, though. He propped himself on his elbows, then dragged his body into a careful sitting position. It was an unending aggravation to deliberately move like an invalid when the entire rest of his body, aside from his right leg below the knee, not only felt healthy and whole, it felt restless and in need of use as well. But that aggravation was tiny compared to the silence in the room around him.

"Red?" he asked again, as if Red would materialize out of the woodwork or from behind the curtains.

It was clear Red wasn't there. Luc propped himself up a bit more, debating whether Red had run back to his own bedchamber to wash and dress or whether he'd gone in search of a footman or maid, or even breakfast. After a successful day downstairs the day before, Luc had made it known to one and all that he wished to wash and dress and join the others downstairs for activities every day from that point on. Perhaps Red had scarpered off in protest, thinking Luc wouldn't be able to get himself downstairs alone.

If that was what he'd done, then Luc would prove him wrong. He swung his body over to the side of the bed, planted his left foot on the floor, then stood as carefully as he could. His leg had long since stopped stinging with sharp pain, but it did throb whenever he moved it a certain way.

He fought to keep his leg as still as possible as he hobbled his way across the room toward the screen and the chamber pot. Along the way, he grabbed one of the small, wooden chairs Red had brought into the room days before and used that as a sort of crutch to help his progress.

Using the chamber pot was easy enough, so Luc continued on, making his way to the washstand and pulling off his nightshirt so that he could bathe. It was relatively simple to do without Red's help, but he would be a fool if he didn't admit he preferred Red's hands running the sponge all over his naked body to his own. Even the thought of Red's ministrations had his cock waking up.

Luc thought he was in for a treat when he heard the bedchamber door open behind him, and he even went so far as to say, "Oh, good, you're here just in time to scrub my willy."

He nearly leapt out of his skin and broke his leg all over again when Sigglesthorpe, not Red, replied, "I will never turn down an invitation to wash a willy."

Luc started so hard that he dropped the sponge with a wet splat on the floor. He had to twist around and sit heavily in the chair he'd been using as a prop to keep himself from losing his balance and falling. That, of course, ended with him on full display to Sigglesthorpe as he splayed his legs to both protect his broken leg and find his balance.

Sigglesthorpe was no gentleman. His eyes went straight to Luc's flagging cock, and he made a humorously scandalized sound before slapping a hand over his eyes. "I cannot look," he declared with all of the drama of Sarah Siddons.

Of course, a moment later, he parted his fingers and peeked through them at Luc's crotch.

Luc leaned to one side and reached for a towel on the table, yanking it over to cover himself. "What in God's name are you doing here, Sigglesthorpe?" he asked, unable to stop himself from laughing. "And where is Red?"

"The hour has grown late, and your friends were wondering why you have not yet joined us for breakfast," Sigglesthorpe explained, walking deeper into the room with a careless step. "I volunteered to rouse you in bed." He clapped his fingertips to his mouth, then went on with, "That is, I volunteered to rouse you *from* bed."

Luc laughed harder and shook his head. "Don't let Red hear you saying those things, you ridiculous flirt. He'd have your balls for breakfast."

"Ooh! Yes, please," Sigglesthorpe said in a coquettish voice.

Luc laughed harder and shook his head. Red—and Anthony, for that matter—had warned him that Sigglesthorpe was a flirt, but they'd assured him the man was actually harmless and that he had no designs on men who were truly not interested in him.

Indeed, after the initial play was over, Sigglesthorpe dropped his coy demeanor and moved to sit in the upholstered chair near the fireplace. "I notice that your paramour is not here," he said, arching one eyebrow.

Luc's smile dropped. "Yes, that concerns me. He is usually up before I am, performing his penance by making sure tea is brought up and arranging my shaving things."

"If you'd like, I could do all that for you," Sigglesthorpe volunteered.

Luc shook his head and stood, keeping the towel around him. "I might go without a shave today, since we've no company other than ourselves."

"I do like a rugged man," Sigglesthorpe said, returning to his coquettish ways. "There's just something about a rough face, broad, firm muscles, and a powerful mien that leaves my girlish heart all aflutter."

"From what I've been told, there's something about any man with his cock out that leaves you aflutter," Luc teased him, gesturing for Sigglesthorpe to hand him the clean pair of breeches that Red had set out the night before.

Sigglesthorpe followed suit, saying, "One cannot help but desire what he desires." After Luc took the garments, Sigglesthorpe made an off-hand gesture and said, "I discovered at an early age what I liked, and that I was not afraid to get it. If I were a man who pursued women, my fellows would laugh and slap me on the back and congratulate me for being a fine, virile man. I would be celebrated by my peers. Why should the same not be so with my pursuit of other men? Where are my congratulations for spreading my arse for every strapping fellow to enjoy with the same frequency as a celebrated buck visits his half-dozen mistresses' beds?"

"Where indeed?" Luc asked with a broad grin as

he donned his modified breeches. The more he came to know Lord Sigglesthorpe, the more he surprised himself by admiring the peacock. And why shouldn't he flaunt his desires as openly as any other man? He should have that right. They all should. "That does not answer my question, though," he said as Sigglesthorpe brought him a clean shirt. "Where is Red?"

"I do not know any more than you do," Sigglesthorpe said, moving in front of Luc to help him finish dressing. "We all assumed he was ensconced here with you."

Through his worry for Red, Luc managed to peek up at Sigglesthorpe and say, "You do realize I am in no way interested in dallying with you."

Sigglesthorpe grinned. "Of course you are not. You have Redmond. I will never pass up an opportunity to hone my skills, though," he added, tying Luc's neck-cloth as Luc tucked his shirt into his breeches. "Flirting is my favorite pastime."

"Yes, I've noticed," Luc laughed. "Would you mind calling the footmen?"

"I will call them whatever you'd like, ducky," Sigglesthorpe answered with a wink.

Luc's concern for Red lasted through finishing dressing and grooming, and as the footmen arrived to convey him downstairs. As nice as it was to know he had a helpful and amusing friend in Sigglesthorpe, the only man he wanted to think about was Red.

Red wasn't in the breakfast room with the others when Luc was brought in and placed in a chair at the end of the table, a second chair for his leg arranged beside him.

"The two of you didn't have a falling out, did you?" Barrett asked as they all puzzled over the matter across the table.

"No," Luc said, nodding to the footman who served his breakfast. "In fact, I'd finally convinced him to sleep in the bed last night instead of that chair on the other side of the room." He was suddenly deeply aware that Haight sat at the table with them—though the man looked distracted by his thoughts—and added, "It was the least bit of comfort I could offer after the way Red has been so attentive of my injury this last week."

The others peeked at Haight to see if he understood the deeper meaning of what had been said as well. For the moment, it seemed as though Haight wasn't paying attention and they were in the clear.

"It isn't at all like Red to run off without telling anyone where he has gone," Anthony mused from the head of the table.

"I am afraid Lord Beverley's absence is my fault," Haight said, glancing up and proving that he was paying attention after all. "We met in the study deep into the night when neither of us could sleep. I am afraid that, in the course of conversation, I divulged to him that Oliver was my grandson."

Luc blinked and nearly choked on his tea. The others were startled, but not one of them looked truly surprised.

"You are Oliver Shaw's grandfather?" Luc asked, a twist of incredulity hitting him as the others turned guilty looks his way.

"I am," Haight confessed with a sigh. He glanced to Anthony, then back to Luc as he said, "His Grace deemed it wise for me not to reveal the truth to Lord Beverley, which meant the truth could not be revealed to you either. But the truth is out now."

"How did he take it?" Barrett asked. He, and

everyone else at the table, leaned forward, buzzing with concern.

"Well, I think," Haight said. "He was upset, as we all suspected he would be. But he did not react as fiercely as you all predicted he might."

"Except that he is currently missing," Anthony said, gesturing for one of the footmen to leave what he was doing with the food on the sideboard to come to him. "Robbie, please find Mr. Worthington and inform him that we need to locate Lord Beverley as soon as possible."

"Yes, Your Grace." Robbie bowed, then left the room.

"I can assure you," Haight said, "Lord Beverley did not appear to be any danger to himself. I believe my confession merely gave him a great deal to consider."

"I would wager Red went for a walk to work things through," Luc said, pretending to be at ease in the hope that he actually would calm down and think rationally. "Didn't he used to walk the decks of the *Majesty* in the middle of the night when anything troubled him?"

"He did," Barrett answered, his shoulders dropping in relief.

The rest of them seemed to relax a bit as well.

"Perhaps this is not ideal timing," Haight went on, "but I feel the time has come for me to leave."

Another wave of surprise gripped the table.

"Please do not feel the need to depart because of my brother," Anthony said, his look one of deep concern.

"It isn't that, rest assured." Haight smiled. He sat a bit straighter. "No, it is just that I have come to the conclusion that I will not pursue the purchase of any part of your lovely estate for a factory."

"You've given up on the idea?" Anthony asked.

All eyes at the table bounced between the two of them as their conversation continued.

"I have," Haight confessed. "In truth, as I told Lord Beverley last night, I came to Wodehouse Abbey primarily because I knew that you officers from the *Majesty* were in residence here. I have very much enjoyed spending time with you all, and I thank you, Lord Copeland, and you, Mr. Bolton, especially for the stories of my grandson that you have shared with me."

Luc's brow went up even farther. He had somehow missed out on the information that Haight was Oliver's grandfather, but all this time, the others had been swapping stories of Oliver's time at sea with the man? What had he been doing all that time?

The answer was as obvious as the question. He'd been tangled up with Red, both literally and figuratively. The others hadn't simply stopped existing just because he'd been bedridden and in the throes of a romantic crisis.

"You are welcome to extend your visit as long as you'd like, Mr. Haight," Anthony told the man. "And you are more than welcome to return at any time, even though your interest in purchasing land has ended."

Haight was in the middle of thanking Anthony for his kindness when Worthington appeared in the doorway, a letter in his hand, with Mr. Goddard right behind him. The sight of Goddard brought the feeling of a collective groan with it, even though no one groaned aloud.

"Mr. Goddard, Your Grace," Worthington announced a moment late, glaring at Goddard for entering the room before being announced as he did.

Goddard didn't wait for Worthington to finish before booming, "What is this? You have decided against purchasing the fine property I have lined up for you?"

Luc exchanged a look with Barrett, who, in turn, exchanged a few other looks with Septimus, Spencer, and Clarence.

Anthony rose from his seat. "I beg your pardon, sir." He stared hard at Goddard, utterly unamused with the man's bullishness and lack of manners. "It is far too early for a call."

"Sit down, Goddard," Haight told the man, rising in his place as well. He was clearly just as annoyed as Anthony. "Where are your manners?"

For a moment, Goddard gaped like a fish. Then he dove for the chair that should have been Red's, sitting clumsily. He leaned his forearms inelegantly on the table. "Surely, we can discuss this matter," he said to Haight with an air that Luc was certain he intended to be coaxing, but which, instead, came off as grating. "Do you not remember what I said about the convenience of the location? About the welcome that the community would be certain to show you and your proposed factory for the employment it will create?"

"Yes, Mr. Goddard, I remember," Haight said. "I simply no longer believe this is a suitable property for such things. I have come to enjoy Wodehouse Abbey, and I believe it should remain as it is."

Goddard sputtered in indignation, but as he gathered himself enough to refute Haight's words, Worthington stepped over to Luc leaned close to his ear, and handed him the envelope he carried.

"Forgive me, but the post just arrived on the wagon with Mr. Goddard, and I believe this letter could be something you may want to address immediately," he said.

"Thank you, Worthington," Luc said, examining the letter. It was addressed from the Admiralty.

"Do I need to list all of the reasons why the property of Wodehouse Abbey is ideal for development again?" Goddard demanded of Haight, addressing the older man as though he were a disobedient child.

The others clucked and gasped in disapproval at the man's atrocious manners and horrible attitude. Luc ignored them all, breaking the seal on his letter and opening it. He already knew what it would say, and as it happened, he was right.

Goddard had started his list, but Anthony held up a hand to stop him, staring at Luc instead. "Is it what you feared?" he asked.

The table went silent as Luc finished scanning the letter. At the end, he sighed and folded it once more. "It is," he said. "I have lost command of the *Daphne*. The Admiralty cannot wait for me to recover and assume its captaincy."

A chorus of disappointed and sympathetic sounds around the table met Luc's announcement.

"There is more," he went on, feeling strangely lighter than he assumed he would feel at the demise of his hopes and dreams. "Because the Admiralty is aware that injuries such as mine often result in long-term difficulties, they have moved my name to the bottom of the list of officers seeking new commissions, and they recommend I withdraw my name from consideration entirely and pursue a different occupation."

More sympathy echoed around the table.

"So that's it, then," Red's voice sounded from the doorway. He was dressed in nothing but his banyan and nightshirt, and his bare feet and calves were sandy, as though he'd gone for a walk on the beach—and probably fallen asleep there, given the late hour and his current, disheveled state. It was his bereft expression that caught Luc's attention and squeezed his heart, though. "I've thoroughly ruined your life," he went on. "And there isn't a damned thing anyone can do about it."

17

It seemed as though the self-loathing Red had danced with for so many months now only ever grew worse each time he thought he'd mastered it. The force of darkness within him felt like an iron grip from an outside source, a part of him that wasn't truly him. It felt as though it would never let him go. It tightened it's hold once again as he stood in the doorway of the breakfast room and listened to Luc tell the others that his career with the Navy, his life as he knew it, was over.

"Red." Luc shifted to face him, distress painted clearly in the strong, handsome lines of his face. The distress was not for himself, as it should be. Luc was anxious on Red's behalf. The man's world was falling down around him, but still his concern was for Red. It was too much to bear.

"No." Red shook his head. "I cannot do this to you anymore. You have sacrificed too much for an unworthy soul like me, and now I've ruined the rest of your life. But I won't anymore."

He turned and strode out of the room, probably trailing sand across the hall from his retreat to the beach. The floor was just one more thing that he would damage with his recklessness.

"Redmond, stop." This time, it was Anthony's voice that followed him into the hall, and it was filled with the sort of command that marked Anthony as the duke that he was.

Red turned to face his brother, ready to argue and insist that he didn't deserve the attention or the consideration he was getting. To his surprise, Anthony wasn't alone. A few steps behind him, Clarence carried Luc out into the hall.

"I refuse to let you walk away from me yet again," Luc said, in spite of the fact that he was being carried like a baby and the rest of their friends had gotten up from the table to poke their heads into the hall as well. Luc faced Red as though the two of them were alone. He nudged Clarence to carry him closer to Red. "You have not destroyed my life," he went on in a softer voice, "you have made it wonderful."

"What the devil is going on here?" Goddard asked, stomping into the hall behind the others. "Have I walked in on a scene from Bedlam? And why will you not address my very real concerns over the land deal that you have so obviously stolen from me so that you can profit on your own?"

Goddard's petty fussing was so incongruous to Red's deep, emotional turmoil that for a moment he had no idea what to think. His heart ached with love and regret, his head was completely done in with grief and melancholia, but in that very moment, for some ungodly reason, the sight of Luc clasped in Clarence's massive arms, his grip tight around Clarence's neck, his splinted leg dangling awkwardly to one side, coupled with the nuisance that was Goddard made him want to laugh. Perhaps Goddard was right after all and it was a scene from Bedlam.

Anthony shifted slightly, drawing Red's attention. He stood straighter, frowned, then pointed at Red. "You. In the conservatory with Luc. It is time you sorted this ridiculous nonsense about you ruining everyone's lives. Now." He turned to Goddard, also glancing to Haight briefly before focusing on Goddard again. "You. In the morning parlor with Mr. Haight and myself to discuss the matter of the land sale, once and for all. The rest of you would do well to find ways to occupy yourselves that do not involve interfering with the lives of others."

"Where is the fun in that?" Percy asked, a twinkle in his eyes, his shoulders slumping with disappointment.

Anthony narrowed his eyes at Percy. "Lord Sigglesthorpe, why are you still here? I still do not recall inviting you to Wodehouse Abbey to begin with or giving you leave to extend your visit."

"Perhaps I will take a turn around your beautiful gardens," Percy whispered, his face going pink, his eyes still flashing with mischief. He peeled away from the others and hurried off down the hall.

Anthony turned back to Red. "Go. Resolve whatever this is between you."

"Go ahead," Luc murmured to Clarence. "I need to sit down properly anyhow."

Luc's suggestion that he was uncomfortable was all it took to motivate Red to move. He followed as Clarence carried Luc to the conservatory at the back of the house. As soon as Clarence settled Luc on one of the long sofas near the French doors that looked out to the garden, he bowed with exaggerated ceremony, then executed a turn with military precision and marched out of the room.

"I think Clarence is enjoying the theatrics of the morning a little too much," Luc said, entirely too close to laughing for Red's comfort.

"Please," Red said, falling into the chair beside the sofa. He leaned forward, resting his elbows on his knees, and rubbed his face. "Please stop pretending as though everything is just a game and that it doesn't matter if you're losing."

Luc was in the middle of adjusting his splinted leg, but at Red's words he stopped and snapped straight. "I thought that you were the one who believed everything was simply a game."

There was an edge of frustration in Luc's voice that caused Red to peek through his fingers, then to lower his hands from his face entirely. "Perhaps that is what has led to this mess I am in now," he said, his chest squeezing with the truth of things. "I have treated life as a game, and I have lost that game."

"In what way have you lost?" Luc laughed at him, but Red could hear the frustration within his laughter. "You are the son of a duke. You earned a title of your own through your acts of service and bravery during the war. You will never want for anything. You have a brother who loves you, friends who admire you, and, if you just say the word, a lover who would adore you for the rest of your days." He lowered his voice to a tender whisper with his last words and reached a hand toward Red.

Red's heart ached and twisted. "It seems so bloody unfair," he sighed, rubbing his face again instead of taking Luc's hand. "What sort of justice is it that I have been given so much while Shaw and all the others have had everything taken away from them, including their lives?"

Luc pulled his hand back and crossed his arms. "Haight told us that the two of you had a conversation last night. Is it true he is Shaw's grandfather?"

Red glanced up from his hands in surprise. "You didn't know either?"

Luc shrugged and shook his head. "I did not. I only just found out the truth. What did he say to you that would cause you to rush off to the beach," he nodded at Red's sandy calves and banyan, "in the middle of the night?"

Red drew in a long breath and pushed back, flopping into the chair. "He said that he forgives me." His voice broke with the confession and the way it made him feel. "He told me he never blamed me to begin with, that nobody does. He said it was young Oliver's time."

"Haight is an extraordinary man," Luc said solemnly.

"Oliver Shaw could have been as well," Red agreed, blinking back tears. God, he'd been convinced he was through with weeping, but there it was again, emotion so acute it squeezed his throat and made him feel as though he would never be free of its grip. "So could you have been," he added, sending a mournful glance to Luc, "if I had not shattered your leg and your chances for greatness."

To Red's surprise, and a bit of annoyance, Luc laughed out loud. "You think so little of me that you believe I cannot be great unless it is with an undamaged body, while in command of a ship?"

Sheepish heat flooded Red's face. "That is not what I meant at all," he said, squirming a bit as he sought to find a comfortable way to sit. "I dare say you

will be successful and celebrated for whatever endeavor you pursue."

"Then for God's sake, man, why must you persist
in flogging yourself for every little wrong that has happened in your vicinity?" Luc demanded.

"Because I am a disgrace," Red said. For the first
time, however, the words didn't sink into his soul the
way they always had before in times when he'd contemplated his mistakes. They felt like a recitation he'd
been compelled to speak over and over, but that was
beginning to feel pointless.

Luc didn't even reply. He merely tilted his head
and arched one eyebrow, as if inviting Red to come to
his own conclusions on the subject.

The strange thing was, after everything Haight had
said to him the night before, after the thoughts that
had swirled through his head during his walk along
the beach—and the fact that he'd fallen asleep in a
sheltered spot on the sand and dreamed of nothing at
all until the sun and seagulls woke him—and after the
rapport he and Luc had developed in the last week
and the way it had strengthened their bond, Red
didn't need Luc to say a word in order to feel the
weight of the point his lover was making.

"Come here," Luc said at last, his tone conveying
nothing but tenderness and compassion.

Red peeked uncertainly at him, hesitated for a few
seconds, then slipped off the chair. He shifted to sit on
the edge of the sofa beside Luc. At last, he took the
hand Luc had offered him before.

"Why is it so difficult for you to believe that you
are not to blame for Shaw's accident?" Luc asked. Red
noted well the change in referring to the event as
"Shaw's accident" instead of "Shaw's death". "Why do
you think a slip with a pall-mall mallet during a game,

when we were both under a great deal of duress, represents the ruination of my career and my life?"

"Because—" Red began, but wasn't certain what to say after. "Because—" He tried again, but still nothing came out.

The trouble was, for the first time, he could feel the truth rising up through his spine and curling around his heart. He could feel the thing he'd been laughing at and running from, the things he'd been trying to get away from by playing games and fucking, as though they were all one bubble that was finally about to burst.

"Because I don't understand why I am here when Shaw isn't. Countless men died, Luc, but we lived. Why?" he asked, tears stinging his eyes again. "What was the purpose of the war to begin with? To stop Bonaparte? To seek revenge for the aristocratic victims of the guillotine? So that men even higher than us can make a grab for land? Because of other men's greed, Oliver Shaw will never come home. So many of the men we served with, the ones we fought against too, lost their lives, their futures, and for what?"

Luc let out a breath and reached for Red, pulling him into his arms and holding him close. "War is a terrible thing, my love," he said, resting his cheek against the top of Red's head. "But every one of us joined the cause of our own free will. We believed in something, even if it seems like a false god now, and we all knew, even young Shaw, that death in the service of the king was a real possibility."

"It all seems so senseless now," Red said, closing his eyes and leaning heavily against Luc. The heat of his body, his familiar scent, and the steady rhythm of his heart under Red's cheek was the balm that Red had been seeking for his soul for what felt like forever.

"As senseless as a missed swing with a pall-mall mallet ending your dreams of sailing around the world."

Luc stiffened, pushing Red back so that he could gape at him. "Is that what you thought my dream was?" he asked.

"It's what you always spoke about," Red said, confused as to why Luc suddenly seemed incredulous. "All those times we had too much rum on shore leave or stared out from the aft deck of one ship or another, watching the sun set over the horizon. You always talked about sailing around the world, seeing the ports of India or the Dutch East Indies or Cathay. You talked about us circumnavigating the globe, though I will admit that could have been a euphemism for something else."

Luc grinned, resting a warm hand on the side of Red's face. "Oh, it was absolutely a euphemism," he said, then surprised Red with a kiss. It was short and with closed mouths, but it rocked Red to his foundation. Especially when Luc went on to say, "It wasn't about sailing, Red. It never was. It was about the two of us together. I couldn't care less if we were bound to the grounds of Wodehouse Abbey for the rest of our lives, or even if we were forbidden from leaving the house, as long as the two of us are together."

Those words struck Red deeper than anything he'd ever heard before. They gave him hope.

All the same, he arched a sly eyebrow and said, "Surely, you wouldn't want to be limited to the house alone. You adore being out of doors."

"I do," Luc agreed, stealing another, short kiss that left Red aching for more. "But I would give up even sunshine and fresh air for you, Red. That is why I accepted your invitation to convalesce here for the summer instead of staying in Portsmouth—which you must admit would have been decidedly more practical if my heart was truly set on returning to sea alone."

Red blinked, his brow lifting. "I had never considered that."

"I've only ever just wanted to be near you," Luc went on, "to be with you in every way. That is why this last week has been one of the happiest of my life, in spite of the pain in my leg. And the pain in my arse, I might add, which is unequivocally you. Dragging you out of this morass of melancholia has taken far more effort than it should have."

"I'm sorry," Red said. His face twitched, as he didn't know whether to beam with joy or grimace with guilt. Every word that came from Luc's lips lifted his heart and made him feel as though he might just be able to overcome the torment that the war had left him with after all, but he still wasn't entirely convinced he deserved such wonderful things. Not when he really was to blame for Luc's injury, and probably for a great many things besides.

Luc adjusted so that he could clasp both hands on the sides of Red's face and stare longingly into his eyes. "It was never just about fucking for me. Not now and not ever. You know that, do you not?"

Red's heart pinched with a new kind of guilt and regret, a kind that went even deeper than the responsibility for Shaw and the others who had died in the war. He'd treated Luc so unfairly in his efforts to assuage that lesser guilt—treated him like any other pretty boy who waited anxiously by the docks when he saw ships coming in so that he could make a penny or two. Luc was so much more than a bit of arse or a lad to play games with. He was everything Red had been waiting to embrace once the war was over.

"It wasn't just about scratching an itch for me either," he said, clasping the side of Luc's face as well. "It never will be."

"I'm glad we've sorted that out," Luc said, his eyes glittering with love and mirth.

Before Luc could get another word out, Red leaned into him, capturing his mouth in a kiss that expressed all of the longing and love, and a good deal of the regret, that he'd felt for so long. He wasted no time coaxing Luc to part his lips so that they could dive into each other, tongues dancing in the only game that was truly worth playing and winning.

"I love you, Red," Luc gasped between kisses as Red leaned into him even more. He threaded his fingers through Red's hair with one hand and dropped the other to tug at the tie of Red's banyan. "I've never loved anyone the way I love you."

Red made a sound at the back of his throat, but he was too caught up in kissing Luc to form it into words. He needed to drink Luc in, to let the man's goodness seep into him and make him whole again. The two of them had made it through the war together. Naturally, the only way they could continue on to make a life after the war was together as well.

He was on the verge of thanking God that he only wore a banyan and nightshirt, his hands moving to the buttons of Luc's jacket, when Percy burst into the doorway.

"You'd better move apart," he warned them, eyes wide. He peeked back into the hall, then stared at Red and Luc again. "They're coming this way. Goddard is already in a temper and promising revenge. Don't give him any more ammunition."

Goddard could go to hell, as far as Red was concerned, but he had no inclination whatsoever to land Luc in any more trouble than he was already in. He wasn't fast enough to move away from Luc or to right the mess they'd made of their clothes, though.

"It is an outrage, I tell you," Goddard's voice was heard shouting before Anthony entered the room with Haight, as though shepherding the man to somewhere that might be safe from the man's wrath. "This is highway robbery, you can be sure," Goddard continued as he turned the corner into the room. "I will not rest until I am compensated for your treachery, sir."

Haight seemed mostly irritated as he stepped into the conservatory with Anthony, but as soon as he saw the position and the state Red and Luc were in, his expression popped into one of surprise.

18

A part of Luc was so filled with bliss at the new level of understanding he and Red had reached that he didn't care if Mr. Haight or all the world saw the love that existed between them. Surely, after spending nearly a fortnight at Wodehouse Abbey, Mr. Haight must have sensed the connections between the men living or staying in the house was not what society would have considered ordinary.

All the same, as the drama that had begun outside of the breakfast room funneled into the conservatory, Luc did his best to sit straighter, refasten the buttons of his jacket, and attempt to hide the noticeable bulge in his breeches.

"No one has robbed you in any way, Mr. Goddard." Anthony turned his thunderous expression on Goddard as he marched away. It was almost as if Goddard believed Anthony would attempt to have him tossed from the house, so he was attempting to stay as far away from him as possible. "As I understand it, Haight made you no promises to purchase my land—which I will remind you was not up for sale to begin with."

"I am not quite certain I understand where your obsession with my purchase of His Grace's land originated to begin with," Haight added, dragging his gaze away from Luc and Red. He took a second look, understanding dawning in his expression, before shaking his head slightly and giving his attention to Goddard. "Our arrangement was for me to view the land, and for you to suggest other possible locations in this part of Yorkshire as well, which you have failed to do, I might add. But His Grace's invitation to stay at Wodehouse Abbey as a guest and my connection to the officers of the *Majesty* changed all that."

"But this is the perfect location upon which to build a factory, sir," Goddard insisted. "Not to mention that my commission from the purchase of the land would have enabled me to—"

He stopped abruptly, causing Luc to frown and study him. Luc wasn't the only one. A ripple of suspicion passed through the room. Goddard had been up to something, but whatever it was had failed.

"Your Grace, I am terribly sorry that my presence has caused such a commotion in your house," Haight said. "And at such a time when the young men in residence are seeking to recover from the strains of the war." He glanced straight at Red with a sympathetic look as he spoke. "I am afraid I have overstayed my welcome, and, as I have had the conversations that I came here hoping to have, I trust you will allow me to pack my things at once and return to London. I am afraid I have neglected my business dealings there long enough."

"As I said earlier, Mr. Haight, you are welcome to stay as long as you'd like, or to return at your leisure," Anthony told the man with a kind nod. "I trust we part as friends."

"We do, Your Grace." Haight nodded in return. "I am honored to call you a friend. I am honored to call

all of you friends." He glanced around the room at the others, smiling particularly at Red, then peeking at Luc again. Fortunately, he continued to smile as he did.

"You and I do not part as friends," Goddard snapped, taking a threatening step toward Haight.

Clarence and Septimus rushed forward to stand between Goddard and Haight.

"Careful there, boy," Clarence growled.

Goddard's eyes went wide. "How dare you address me in such a disrespectful manner. Who are you at any rate?"

"A man you do not want to vex," Clarence said, crossing his arms.

"I should retire to my room at once to pack my things," Haight said in a hushed voice, glancing warily at Goddard.

"Would you allow me to accompany you?" Red asked, gesturing for the doorway and escorting Haight there in anticipation of his answer.

"Yes, thank you, Lord Beverley," Haight said.

Red shot Luc a look over his shoulder that said their conversation was far from over as he escorted Haight from the room. He smiled at Red from the bottom of his heart. The power and confidence had returned to his demeanor, which gave hope that the conversation they would end up having would finally set things to right.

But there were other things that needed to be dealt with first.

As soon as Haight was out of the room, Anthony rounded on Goddard as though he were an avenging angel. "You, sir, have set foot in my house for the very last time," he said. He took a threatening step toward the man. "You have come uninvited more often than I should have allowed you to. I have been lenient up until this point, but I cannot allow this manner of disrespect to continue. Your behavior toward me, toward my staff, and toward my guests could be described as criminal. If you set foot on the grounds of Wodehouse Abbey again, I will call the constable and have you arrested for trespassing."

"And I will have you arrested for buggery, Your Grace," Goddard hurled back at him.

Luc flinched slightly—not because of the accusation, but because Goddard had more or less thrust his hand into a hornet's nest.

"Worthington," Anthony called out, showing no reaction to Goddard's accusation whatsoever. Worthington instantly appeared around the corner, as if he'd been waiting for orders. "Please see Mr. Goddard out."

"With pleasure, Your Grace." Worthington nodded, then moved toward Goddard.

"Oh, no," Goddard said, holding up his hands to the butler. "You will not throw me out as though I am a piece of rubbish. And you will not deny me the fortune I stand to make by the sale of part of this property," he hurled at Anthony.

"What makes you think that I would even begin to consider carving up an ancient estate such as this for your profit, sir?" Anthony demanded as he closed in on Goddard.

"Because I know the truth, Your Grace," Goddard nearly shouted as, between Worthington and Anthony, he was pushed from the room. "I know that you are harboring a gang of criminals at Wodehouse Abbey, and once the truth comes out, you will be forced to sell your land, regardless of your intentions, to pay your legal fees."

"Clarence," Luc called to his friend as he swung his legs over the edge of the sofa and tried hurriedly to stand on his own. "Help me to keep up with them."

Clarence's expression had brightened into pure amusement. He'd already started toward the doorway, following the rest of the company, but he veered to the side to pick Luc up and carry him again.

"Did you ever imagine that convalescing in a quiet country house in Yorkshire would feel so much like living inside of a Moliere comedy?" he asked, full of humor, as he carried Luc out into the hall in pursuit of the drama. "We should slam a few doors to make the appearance complete."

"I cannot tell if I would prefer that we actually had peace and quiet or if this interlude is exactly the sort of entertainment we need to amuse ourselves," Luc laughed as Clarence carried him on.

Goddard evidently didn't think there was anything amusing in the way he had been summarily pushed down the hall and out through the front door onto the gravel drive that looped past the front of the house. "You cannot continue to harbor fugitives this way forever, Your Grace," he roared at Anthony as the two faced each other on the stairs of the marble terrace that led from the front door to the drive. "The law will find you, and when it does, you will beg me to find a buyer for not just part of your estate, but all of it."

"What in God's name are you talking about, man?" Barrett shouted back, taking up a place by Anthony's side. "Have you lost your mind? There are no criminals or fugitives from justice at Wodehouse Abbey."

Instead of backing down or slinking off with his tail between his legs, as he should have, Goddard's eyes took on an almost manic light. "That is what you think," he said, glancing from Anthony to Barrett to the rest of them in turn, "but you are all wrong. I know what has transpired on this estate, and I will stop at nothing until the truth comes out." The man glanced straight to Clarence and Luc, narrowing his eyes.

Luc wasn't certain why, but something in the back of his mind told him that whatever delusion Goddard was operating under, it extended far more than the fact that the vast majority of the men in residence at the Abbey preferred the company of other men. In his experience, in spite of the law, a vast number of people were more than happy to look in the other direction when faced with what they saw as an awkward truth, as Haight had just demonstrated minutes before. Particularly if they had no dealings with the men in question whatsoever. Goddard was enough of a man of the world to know that. He had to believe something else was afoot.

That theory took root even deeper when their entire, mad scene was interrupted as the slight and shy young man carrying a hawk on one arm and a book in his other hand rounded the corner of the house. He stopped dead when he saw the assembly on the stairs. The manor house was huge, and the young man was at least thirty yards away from them still, but he instantly looked as though he wanted to turn and run.

Curiously, Spencer flushed at the sight of the young man. That was enough for Luc to break into a smile, in spite of the chaos of the situation. The young man had to be Declan Shelton, the gamekeeper, who Spencer had mentioned in glowing tones during one of his visits to Luc's room in the past week.

Evidently, Goddard knew who the young man was as well. "Ah ha!" he called out, pointing toward Declan. "You see?" he demanded, as if the young gamekeeper's presence alone was proof of criminal activity.

"What does the son of my land steward have to do with your mad accusations?" Anthony asked, clearly at his wit's end.

"Criminals, all of you," Goddard said. "When the constable finds out, you'll be in a sorry state."

Goddard started toward Declan, as though he would draw the young man into the conflict. Before he could take more than a handful of crunching steps across the gravel of the drive, the hawk on Declan's arm launched into the air and flew at Goddard, screeching. Goddard screamed and dropped into a crouch, covering his head with his arms, even though the hawk didn't fly anywhere near him.

Even Luc flinched at the hawk's swooping flight and screech. Clarence—who was still holding him, even when he could easily had put Luc down—tensed as well and let out a string of curses that Luc hadn't heard since their days on the *Hawk*. He blinked, then laughed at the irony of being startled by the bird their ship had been named after.

"Get it away from me, get it away from me," Goddard cried from his crouched position on the driveway.

To Luc's surprise, Haight leaned out of a window on the second floor and shouted, "For God's sake, man! Can you not simply leave a place where you are no longer welcome without causing such an almighty fuss? What is the matter with you?"

Goddard pushed himself to stand, indignation rippling off of him. "I shall bring you up on charges in this matter as well, Mr. Haight," he shouted. "Breech of contract, broken business dealings, all of it!"

Luc shook his head. The man was clearly unbalanced to take the loss of a business transaction that was only ever imaginary to begin with so much to heart.

"You will do no such thing, sir," Haight called back to him. "I may be departing Hull today, but before I do, I plan to stop by the offices of Hamilton, Bradley, and Associates to inform them of your erratic behavior."

As he spoke, something shiny slipped from his hand, catching the sunlight as it fell to the grass under his window. Haight muttered something that sounded suspiciously like the sort of curse Clarence had just let out, then pulled back into the house.

"Do not worry, sir. I will fetch it," Worthington called up to the window, heading to the spot under the window.

"No!" Goddard shot forward, cutting Worthington off. "Whatever Haight dropped should be mine. It is the least I deserve for everything that I have done on the man's behalf. Everything I have done, I have done without payment."

"Everything you've done has been with greed and the promise of a future fortune in mind, you mean," Barrett called after him. He turned to Anthony, shaking his head. "Can we not have the man removed forcibly from the property? He is clearly mad. Are there footmen available for the job?"

"I'll gladly take care of the lout," Septimus said, rolling up his shirtsleeves. He hadn't been wearing a jacket at their informal breakfast, and he hadn't bothered to find one once the chaotic scene had begun. The result was that he looked every bit the fisherman's son that he was rather than the lord or gentlemen that most of the rest of them were.

"Have a care," Luc said as Septimus moved toward Goddard—who was attempting to wriggle out of whatever hold Worthington had him in. "The man is clearly touched in the head. Thwarted greed can do that to a man," he said to Clarence, trying not to laugh. Part of him believed Goddard deserved to be laughed at, after the way he'd been behaving, but too much of him simply felt sorry for the man.

A minute or so later, as Septimus took over from Worthington in his attempts to restrain Goddard, Haight strode out of the house, followed by Red.

"Goddard, desist with this madness at once," Haight shouted from the top of the steps, where Clarence still stood.

Luc nudged him to put him down once Red was there to shore up Luc's other side. It felt a thousand times better to stand leaning against Red, even though being upright for so long made Luc's leg throb, than it did to have Clarence carrying him like an invalid. That also freed Clarence to join the fray with Goddard. Spencer had descended the steps and crossed the lawn to where Declan stood at the other end of the yard. Declan's hawk had perched on one of the decorative plinths at the edge of the terrace.

"He claims we're all criminals," Luc commented to Red, nodding to Goddard with a grin that he simply couldn't suppress, no matter how much he knew he should. "He says your brother is harboring fugitives on his property, and that as soon as the law discovers as much, he'll need to sell the estate to pay his way out of jail. At least, I believe that is what he is claiming. I'm not quite certain anymore. It's all madness."

"This is preposterous," Haight hissed, shaking his head. He moved away from Luc and Red, climbing down the steps and starting across the drive toward Goddard. "Enough," he called out to the man. "It is time for you to leave."

"This is your doing as much as it is theirs," Goddard growled, breaking away from Septimus.

As he hurled himself at Haight, Declan's hawk took flight again, then dove straight at Goddard. Once again, Goddard screamed, only this time, instead of diving for the ground, he darted toward Haight. With a second scream, he grabbed Haight with both hands and thrust the older man in front of him like a shield.

"Hermes, no!" Declan shouted, breaking into a run, Spencer by his side.

The hawk shrieked and pulled up, but not before diving so close toward Haight that the older man shouted and raised his arms to bat the hawk away. The rest of them cried out as well, and everyone who was close enough to Goddard and Haight leapt forward in an attempt to help.

The whole thing happened too fast for Luc to see, but as the hawk peeled away and shot back into the sky, Haight and Goddard crashed to the ground.

"Mr. Haight!" Red cried out, surging forward. He let go of Luc, but Luc was able to catch his balance and hobble to one side of the terrace, leaning against the low wall so that he didn't fall.

He watched as Red tore across the gravel of the drive and onto the lawn, where Haight and Goddard lay. Goddard twisted and scrambled to get away and to stand and dash to the side—where Septimus caught him in a grip he wouldn't be able to get away from—but Haight lay still and pale in the grass.

19

The memory hit Red like a cudgel. The one detail that had always been present in his dreams but that he'd never paid attention to flashed through his mind as he watched the scene unfold. His heart stopped, as Declan's hawk, Hermes, dove, screeching, toward Haight and Goddard. Birds. There had been birds circling around the top of the foremast when Oliver Shaw climbed up in the rigging that fateful day. He and Billy had scrambled up with a heel of bread so that they could toss crumbs into the air and watch the gulls swoop in to snap them up. They'd run out of bread, but the birds hadn't gone away. They'd continued to squawk and swoop, demanding more, and in the end, their aggression had caused Shaw to lose his footing and fall, even though Billy had tried his best to hold onto him.

All of that struck Red in a single second, like a lightning bolt that broke a dead branch off a tree. The missing pieces of his memory clicked into place. Shaw hadn't been careless, he'd been attacked. Red hadn't been negligent; he'd sent the older midshipman up with Shaw to mind him. It changed everything, but in the moment, it didn't matter.

"Mr. Haight," he shouted as he tore down the steps, the loose fabric of his banyan threatening to tangle around his legs. "Mr. Haight, are you well?"

He'd run straight to Shaw on that fateful morning as well, reaching him first and scooping the boy's lifeless, broken body into his arms. Everyone had rallied around to do their best to save the boy, but it wasn't to be.

Haight was twice as big as his grandson and apparently unbroken, but Red dropped to his knees, skidding across the grass and ruining his banyan and nightshirt as he did. He then pulled the man into his arms the same way he'd held Shaw.

"Mr. Haight, are you well?" he asked again, resting a hand on the older man's cheek. "Somebody fetch a doctor," he shouted to the stunned friends around him.

He didn't wait to see if his order was obeyed. He gazed down at Mr. Haight and tapped his cheeks lightly in an effort to wake him up. The man was pale, but he seemed unharmed. The hawk hadn't scratched him, he had merely startled him. But that didn't mean he hadn't startled Haight badly enough to stop his heart.

"You see?" Goddard demanded as he tried to wriggle free of Septimus's strong arms. "This estate is filled with nothing but murderers and thieves. But you cannot escape justice forever."

"You will be quiet," Anthony roared at Goddard, crossing first to glare directly into the blackguard's eyes, then continuing on and kneeling beside Red and Haight. "Is he alive?" Anthony asked cautiously.

As if in answer to the question, Haight stirred and groaned. Red could have shouted with joy at that proof that the man's heart hadn't stopped after all. It was likely that he'd merely fainted. He smiled at Haight as the man shook himself, then blinked his eyes open, glancing around in confusion about the position he found himself in. Then Red looked back over his shoulder at Luc, who was cautiously making his way down the terrace steps. Barrett—who had leapt away, along with Worthington, when Red called for a doctor—veered off to help Luc join the group.

"I...I do believe I am still alive," Haight said in a weak voice that still managed to have a touch of humor to it. "Though I am dreadfully embarrassed to have fainted because of a bird."

"The beast should be destroyed," Goddard growled, trying once again to wriggle free from Septimus's grip. "It is a menace and a danger to good people."

Percy laughed out loud at Goddard's words, but the rest of them, Red included, merely glared at him.

"There is nothing wrong with Hermes," Declan insisted in a surprisingly strong voice, from what little Red knew of the shy man's personality. The hawk had returned to perch dutifully on his arm. Hermes blinked and cocked his head to one side, as if baffled by the suggestion that he had done anything wrong. "He was protecting Mr. Haight."

"That monster with feathers does not even know Mr. Haight," Goddard said.

"Not true," Haight said, groaning a bit as he extracted himself from Red's arms and tried to stand.

"Please, sir," Red insisted. "Stay seated until the doctor is fetched to ascertain your health."

"Nonsense." Haight pushed out of Red's cautious hold and stood. Red stood with him. "I am not so old and frail that I cannot recover from a mere faint. Though I do appreciate your concern for my person."

He smiled at Red once they were both standing, then turned to address the others. "I am acquainted with Hermes," he went on, nodding to the hawk on Declan's arm. "During my stay here, I have developed the habit of walking the grounds in the morning. You caught me doing so yourself one morning, Lord Beverley."

"I did," Red admitted.

"During those walks, I was fortunate enough to make the acquaintance of young Mr. Shelton here and his hawk," Haight continued. "He is a fine and noble bird."

Declan lowered his head slightly and smiled, which was all the confirmation Red needed that Haight was telling the truth. Red also noted that a slight look of alarm had come over Declan with Haight's confession that he frequently walked the grounds of the estate, and if Red wasn't mistaken, the young man shot a worried look to Spencer before schooling his expression to neutrality. And Spencer blushed.

The moment was forgotten as Haight finished with, "I agree that Hermes was merely protecting a man who he sees as a friend from assault." He ended by staring hard at Goddard.

"Assault?" Goddard shifted anxiously, his eyes darting around to everyone staring at him, as though he finally realized the weakness of his position. "It was not assault, it was an accident. I...I was merely trying to prove a point to Mr. Haight, and...and..." His mouth hung open as he failed to come up with an excuse.

Even if he had invented the cleverest excuse in the world, Red wouldn't have wanted any part of it. "An accident?" he asked, taking a small step forward and glaring incredulously at the man.

Luc and Barrett had reached their group on the lawn. Red sent his lover a long look, as if he could sort his thoughts and give himself courage to say what had needed to be said for months with a single glance between them. His heart seemed to grow within him as his mind caught up to exactly what Luc had been trying to tell him for weeks.

He turned back to Goddard. "Your rash actions and your selfishness are no accident, sir," he snapped. "An accident is when misfortune occurs in spite of their being no malice or vicious forethought involved. An accident is something that cannot be helped, something we would have fought with everything we have to reverse if we knew it was coming. No matter the consequences, we cannot blame ourselves for genuine accidents." He glanced from Luc to Haight. "I know that now."

His entire chest ached, and his body felt charged with energy to the point where he began trembling slightly. It was the shock of letting go of a weight that had kept him pressed down and low for so long, but that he had suddenly been relieved of. He could see it now. Shaw's death truly was an accident. If he had known the sea birds would distract him, then he would have prevented him and Billy from climbing into the rigging with the bread in the first place. His dreams had jumbled events and caused him to remember the accident incorrectly, to confuse it with a dozen other times Shaw had navigated the rigging perfectly.

And if he had known the game that resulted in Luc's broken leg would end in disaster, he never would have taken that swing in the first place. He never would have played the game at all. He hadn't intended to hurt the man he loved more than he loved anyone.

Goddard, however, was another case entirely.

"You have done nothing but interfere with the lives and livelihoods of my friends and my family since we were first introduced, Mr. Goddard," he said. "Your intentions toward us have been anything but accidental. I do not know what sort of malice you have toward us all, but it ends here and it ends now."

"I quite agree," Anthony said. "Worthington," he called out as the butler stood off to the side, giving instructions to one of the footmen, "tell Robbie that while he is fetching the doctor, he should fetch the constable as well."

"This is outrageous," Goddard protested. "I am not the criminal here. I have only ever attempted to deal fairly with you in business and to produce a land sale agreement that will benefit all parties."

"Benefit yourself, you mean," Luc said, wobbling slightly as he stood with Barrett balancing him.

Goddard glared at him, which Red took as a personal offense. Red moved instantly to stand by Luc's side. He slipped an arm around Luc's waist, allowing his lover to lean heavily against him for support. Red saw it as far more than simply shoring Luc up because of his leg. He took their proximity as a declaration that Luc was right, that the two of them belonged together for the rest of their lives, whatever shape those lives would take.

He would have pulled Luc into his arms entirely, kissed him soundly, and finished the conversation the two of them had started in the conservatory, but that was impossible with Haight present, and with Goddard still looking as though he would find a way to rain misery down on them all.

"You will regret ignoring my help in securing all of your futures," Goddard said, narrowing his eyes at both Haight and Anthony. "You will regret the way you have treated me, cast me aside as though I am nothing."

"My dear boy," Percy said, affecting his most coquettish mannerisms, "the fact of the matter is that you *are* nothing. You are below nothing. You have been nothing but a nuisance for my friends, and I, for one, think it is time that you should go."

Anthony crossed his arms. "Are you inviting yourself to be lord of this manor in addition to an unsolicited guest, Sigglesthorpe?"

The rest of them laughed—which was likely exactly what Percy had intended with his comment. Whatever power Goddard might have had in the moment was shattered. Particularly when Clarence barked a jarringly loud laugh.

Goddard narrowed his eyes at him. "You may laugh all you want now, but you cannot escape your sins forever."

Red blinked in surprise as Clarence snapped his mouth shut and looked vaguely worried. It was enough for Red to give Goddard a second look. The man couldn't actually know things the rest of them didn't, could he?

The thought was in and out of Red's mind before he could do anything about it.

"Your Grace, would you like Robbie to fetch the constable?" Worthington asked. "Or should he simply escort Mr. Goddard away from the estate when he fetches Dr. Norris?"

"I've no need for a doctor," Haight insisted. "I am quite well. Though perhaps I could ask for young Robbie's services in packing the rest of my things while I have a cup of tea to recover from the sour taste Mr. Goddard has left me with."

"That sounds like an excellent idea," Anthony agreed. He turned to Goddard. "Leave my property at once."

Goddard looked as though he would stage one final protest, but the wind left his sails before he could do more than open his mouth. "You'll regret this," he said as he turned to start off down the drive.

As he passed Declan and Hermes, the hawk screeched at him, as though taking one final swipe.

Goddard paused and glared at Declan with a ferocity that made Red wince. "You especially will regret this," he shouted, pointing a finger at the young man.

Declan shied away, but managed to look indignant as he did. What surprised Red was that Spencer looked as though he would fly after Goddard and do the man bodily harm.

"Has Spencer developed a tendre for your gamekeeper?" Luc murmured in Red's ear as they watched Goddard sniff and mumble and storm away from them all.

Red turned to Luc. "Do you know, I wouldn't be at all surprised if that is what has happened."

"Do they even know each other?" Luc asked.

"They must," Red replied. "I haven't seen Spencer around the house much in this last week. Spence and I encountered Declan on a walk a fortnight ago. The two must have maintained their acquaintance after that."

Luc hummed, grinning as he studied Spencer where he stood at the edge of the drive, watching Declan, his cheeks still pink. "I believe I approve of that match."

"There is only one match that concerns me now." Red put all thoughts of his friends and their possible romantic entanglements aside and turned to Luc.

"There is only one match and one man that I should have concerned myself with from the beginning."

Luc dragged his eyes away from Spencer and smiled at Red. It was the sort of smile that could have lit up the darkest night, the sort that made Red feel as though he had come home at last, no matter where he was.

"Did you mean what you said about accidents just now?" Luc asked, leaning more heavily into Red.

It occurred to Red that the way Luc leaned could have had as much to do with exhaustion and the condition of his leg after standing up for so long as it could be a sign of affection. "I meant every word of it," he said earnestly. "Witnessing the hawk attempting to protect Mr. Haight reminded me of something else as well." He realized Haight was listening in, so he turned to include the man, and all of his friends, as he went on with, "My memory of Shaw's fall and subsequent death had been lacking an important, forgotten detail until just now. Your grandson did not fall because of his own carelessness or my negligence, sir." He nodded respectfully to Haight. "He fell because he was accosted by a group of sea birds he had been attempting to feed."

"Those things could be vicious," Barrett said, his expression opening as though he, too, had suddenly remembered the birds. "Young Oliver was always fond of and concerned for those birds."

"Oliver was a tender-hearted young man," Haight agreed with a mournful smile. He glanced to Red. "He is not the only one."

"No, he is not," Luc said, smiling at Red.

More than anything in the world, Red wanted to open his heart and pour out all of the love for Luc that he had bottled up for too long. He didn't know why he'd been so blind as to think what he felt for Luc was anything other than the enduring sort of love that poets wrote about. He'd been about to confess as much in the conservatory, before they'd been interrupted, but even now, with Haight standing by, he was prevented from saying what he truly felt.

Somehow, Haight must have known his presence was suddenly an inconvenience.

"Your Grace," he nodded to Anthony, "if you do not mind, I think I shall return to my room so that I may finish packing."

"I will have that tea I promised waiting for you in the morning parlor when you are ready to say your final goodbyes," Anthony replied with a kind smile.

"I think we would all be happy to take one last tea with you," Percy said, approaching Haight and handing him a silver comb—which must have been the object he'd dropped from his window.

"I hope you will allow me to say my goodbye now," Luc said, pushing away from Red enough so that he could face Haight squarely. "I fear this interlude has taxed what little strength I have at the moment, and I need to lie down for a bit."

"Perfectly understandable, Mr. Salterford." Haight nodded to Luc with a smile. "It has been a pleasure coming to know you, and I wish you the speediest of recoveries."

"And I will say goodbye now as well," Red added, his pulse picking up, "as I believe my friend will need assistance returning to his room."

"You are a good and faithful friend," Haight told him with a nod and a smile. That smile said the man wasn't fooled in the least. "I hope you take my words of last night to heart as well, my lord."

"Oh, I have, Mr. Haight, I have indeed," Red insisted. "I am most grateful for our conversation. I hope we will be able to speak again."

"I am certain we will," Haight said with a smile.

"And now," Red said, turning to Luc and attempting, probably in vain, to speak casually, "it is time to return you to the comfort and safety of your bed."

"Thank you for your kind assistance, Lord Beverley," Luc teased him with formality.

Red helped Luc hobble away from the rest of them as they finished their conversation. As far as he was concerned, he couldn't get Luc up to his bedroom fast enough.

20

It was amazing—not to mention damnably frustrating—how quickly Luc's strength had drained away after such a short time standing, but as Red helped him hobble away from the confrontation with Goddard, he was completely exhausted.

At least, he was exhausted in body. His mind and his heart buzzed and swirled with excitement. Everything that Red had said as part of the argument with Goddard had ignited his soul and fueled his hopes as nothing had so far. He could see a real change in Red, and every part of him hoped and prayed that it was permanent.

"This is preposterous," Red said with more life and vigor in his voice than Luc had heard from him since arriving at Wodehouse Abbey. "You're too tired to walk all the way up to your bedchamber like this."

They paused in the spacious front hallway, at the bottom of the grand staircase. "Are you proposing to carry me up to my bedchamber, like I am a fainting bride on our wedding day?" he asked Red with a wide grin.

Red practically glowed as he met Luc's teasing

look with feigned indignation. "Are you saying I cannot do it?"

Joy soared through Luc. The old Red was back. The bright, playful, clever man he'd fallen so deeply in love with was there in front of him once more, as if the hurricane had finally passed and the skies and seas were calm again.

Luc shrugged one shoulder, pretending to be unimpressed. "You aren't Clarence, after all," he said. "Or even Septimus, for that matter."

"I'm far better than either of them," Red insisted.

Luc was on the verge of replying when Red shifted around him, nudging him off his feet, and lifted him as though he were a child. Luc shouted in surprise, the sound turning into a laugh as he clutched Red's neck for support.

"See?" Red asked, his voice strained with the effort of carrying Luc as he started up the stairs. "You're as light as a feather. This is no trouble at all."

Luc continued to laugh as Red made his way laboriously up the stairs. Under more usual circumstances, if Luc's leg hadn't been in an awkward and bulky splint, Red might not have had any trouble carrying him. Red wasn't exactly slight—not like Declan the gamekeeper, or even Adam Seymour. He wasn't even close to being as firm and strapping as Septimus or Clarence, though.

They made it up the stairs all the same, though Red's state of dishabille didn't help them at all.

"I'm surprised you didn't trip on your skirts on those stairs," Luc chuckled as Red shifted his grip on Luc and carried him along the hall to his bedchamber.

"They're not skirts, you twit," he teased Luc, panting a bit more than he should and sweating a bit.

Luc pretended to glance down, although he was

too concerned with maintaining a firm grip on Red's neck and not upsetting his balance to actually see anything. "They look quite dainty and skirt-like to me."

Red sent him a nasty look that had Luc's heart soaring all over again. The two of them had so much to talk about. He wanted to know everything about what Haight had said to Red the night before. He wanted to know what had happened within Red to cause his clear change of heart—whether it was the brief words they had exchanged in the conservatory or their kiss, or if there was something grander that had been at work in Red's soul that had only now flowered into fullness.

He wanted to talk about the future as well, about all of the things the two of them could do together, how they could live their lives, and all of the possibilities that waited for them. More than anything, though, as Red fumbled with the handle of Luc's door—and as Luc batted his hand away and turned the handle himself so they could go inside—he just wanted to be with this happy, free, restored Red.

As soon as they were alone in the room with the door shut, Red carried Luc to the bed and put him down. It would have been romantic, possibly even suggestive, but Red groaned mightily as he settled Luc on the bedcovers, then sank dramatically to his knees and pretended to pass out, slumped over the bed beside Luc.

Luc laughed out loud. "Come on, now, man. You're not that much of a weakling."

"You've gained at least a stone since injuring yourself to the point where you cannot take exercise," Red panted, peeking up at him.

"I have not," Luc protested. "You've grown weak

from fretting and wandering around like a lost soul this past week instead of taking exercise of your own."

His comment had the paradoxical effect of sobering Red. He remained kneeling, but straightened his back and shifted so that he rested between Luc's knees. It would have been a highly erotic position, particularly as Red nudged his knees wider in order to scoot closer to him, but the somberness that washed over Red made the moment poignant instead.

Luc stroked his lover's disheveled hair, then brushed his hand along Red's unshaven jaw. "What went through your mind?" he asked in a soft voice filled with love. "I saw something transform within you during that mad confrontation. What changed things?"

Red rested his hand over Luc's and leaned his cheek into Luc's touch, as though it were a balm to his soul. He closed his eyes for a moment and let out a breath, and a great deal of tension with it.

"I'd forgotten the birds," he said, then opened his eyes and glanced up at Luc. Luc frowned, uncertain what Red was talking about until he said, "How could I forget that Shaw was accosted by a bunch of birds he'd climbed up the mast to feed?"

Luc frowned. "I though you'd told me he and the other midshipmen were messing about in the rigging."

Red tilted his head to the side. "They were, in a manner of speaking. I...I've been having nightmares about that day." He glanced down with a guilty look. "They've been different every night and so vivid and violent that they've jostled me from a sound sleep. That's why I didn't want to share a bed with you." He peeked up at Luc again, his look even guiltier.

Luc drew in a breath. It all made sense now. "I

wouldn't have thought less of you for them, darling," he said, cradling Red's face with both hands and tilting it up to kiss him. "If you'd woken me with those nightmares, I would have held you until they'd gone away."

A tender look of regret creased Red's face. "I think I would have liked that," he said. He paused for a moment in thought, then shook his head. "Regardless, those nightmares lied to me about what happened that day. I remembered things as they'd really happened when Declan's hawk attacked Goddard. Those sea birds caused Shaw to lose his grip on the rigging, but somehow my mind has been telling me a different story, one in which my lack of discipline and command was the cause of Shaw's fall. I've believed the nightmare instead of the reality."

"You cannot be faulted for that," Luc said, brushing his thumbs over Red's cheeks. "Just as you cannot be faulted for finding your way home when so many of our peers did not. It is exactly as you said outside just now. If you had known in advance and been able to have stopped it, you would have. Accidents happen, and we should not suspend our lives with guilt because of them."

"I no longer wish to suspend my life at all," Red said with renewed enthusiasm, kneeling taller and sliding his arms around Luc's waist. "What you said in the conservatory. That is what I want. I don't care how or where, I just want to spend the rest of my life with you, Lucas. Because I love you."

The words were so simple, and yet they were everything that Luc had longed to hear for so long. Not merely because of the words themselves, but because he could see the truth of them in the depth and warmth of Red's eyes. He could feel the love Red had just confessed radiating from him.

"And I love you, Redmond," Luc said, feeling that love pulse through every part of him.

He leaned down, kissing Red with the full force of that love. Their breath mingled, and their mouths fit so perfectly together. Every kiss they'd shared before paled in comparison to the first one after they'd both let go of everything that had held them back and committed fully to each other. The sea didn't matter, neither did any commission or ship Luc might or might not have. All that mattered was Red living together with him forever.

"I think we should continue this conversation in bed," he murmured against Red's eager mouth, pulling him up and leaning back until he collapsed onto his back with Red above him. "And I think you should remove that dirty, old banyan and soiled nightshirt as well."

"Agreed," Red said, his lips spreading into a smile even as he kissed Luc. He pulled all the way back abruptly and stood, hands already on the tie of his banyan. "But be warned, I'm washing my feet and calves before I get anywhere near your sheets, because they are filthy."

Luc laughed, then arched one eyebrow suggestively. "I think I rather like you filthy."

"I should have known," Red said, throwing off his banyan and heading for the washstand.

For a moment, Luc propped himself on his elbows and drank in the sight of Red's naked body as he yanked his nightshirt off and tossed that carelessly aside as well. Red was already hard, and in spite of their earlier banter, he was as fit and glorious as he'd been during their navy days.

"It isn't fair of you to look without giving me something to look at as well," Red told him from the washstand as he poured clean water from the pitcher into the basin.

"I suppose you're right," Luc sighed, pretending it was a chore to undress.

In reality, he did so enthusiastically as Red scrubbed his calves and feet, then quickly washed the rest of his body. As awkward and uncomfortable as it was for Luc to struggle with his clothes and with dragging his splinted leg fully onto the bed while also peeling back the bedclothes, he would have done it a hundred times over to enjoy the feeling of Red's body against his again.

He managed to undress entirely and splay himself on his back, his injured leg surrounded by pillows as buffers for whatever mischief he and Red got up to next, by the time Red was clean and dry.

"I like you this way," Red hummed as he climbed carefully onto the left side of the bed. "I like you all laid out like a delicious feast for me."

Luc laughed deep in his throat and reached for Red. "And I like you this way," he said. "Happy again and relieved of the burdens you've been carrying around for so long."

Red's face grew momentarily serious again as he gently straddled Luc's thighs and leaned down, bracing his arms on either side of Luc's shoulders. "The pain isn't gone entirely," he said with a sad sigh. It was a different sort of sadness than Luc had seen from him since arriving at Wodehouse Abbey. "My heart still mourns for all of the sailors and soldiers who didn't make it home. I cannot forget their sacrifices."

"I wouldn't want you to," Luc said, brushing Red's

hair back from his face. "I won't forget them either. But the best way for us to remember them is to continue to live."

"And to love," Red agreed, lowering himself to kiss Luc.

It was the most wonderful feeling, and Luc drank in Red's kiss as though it were a balm that could heal every hurt he'd ever had. More than that, he kissed Red back as though returning that balm. He slipped his hands around Red's sides, smoothing his way up the muscles of Red's back, then digging his fingertips in as though he would never let go.

"And perhaps come up with a way to provide employment for the sailors and soldiers who are lucky enough to return from the war," Red went on, as though they were having an ordinary conversation instead of growing hard and hot against each other.

Luc laughed, relaxing and letting his arms flop to the side. "What sort of mad scheme is this?" he asked, smiling up at Red, his heart impossibly full.

Red shrugged and shifted to rest his weight against Luc's thighs while trailing his fingertips up and down Luc's chest and stomach in a way that would drive him mad if Red kept it up. "I didn't just go to the beach in the night to destroy a banyan and nightshirt, you know," he said. "I went to think. To think about a great many things, actually. Factories, for one."

"Factories?" Luc's brow shot up. "What a romantic topic of conversation to bring up when you have me so much at your mercy."

Red laughed, brushing his thumbs across Luc's nipples and causing him to suck in a breath. "Haight had some good points about the responsibilities of factory owners," he said. "It was part of our conversation last night. It has me thinking about ways we might establish some sort of industry on the estate of Wodehouse Abbey after all. Not something as monstrous as a cotton mill, mind you," he rushed on. "Something simpler, gentler. Something that would produce the goods England needs while also providing employment for those men returning from the war to lives that have completely changed."

"Do you have something specific in mind?" Luc asked, reaching up to cradle Red's face.

"Not yet," Red said, softening into a smile. "I thought we might come up with an idea together. It would be a joint endeavor, after all. Something the two of us could build in tandem as we build a life together."

"I would like that," Luc said, smiling from his heart. "I would like that very much."

He muscled himself up enough to draw Red into a kiss. Red gave in to it, slanting his mouth over Luc's and sighing with contentment as he did. Their hands roved as their tongues brushed against each other, and soon, every part of them that could was touching.

It was so much better than any of the times the two of them had indulged in each other since Luc's arrival at the Abbey. There was no desperation involved in their mating, no frantic struggle to forget nightmares or desperation to bring the two of them close enough together for a long-overdue confession of love. It was just the two of them, their hearts, their minds, and their bodies finally acting as one and in concert with each other. Even with the limitations of Luc's injury, the two of them were perfect together.

"I love you," Red said over and over as he worshipped Luc's body with kisses. "You are the most wonderful, most loyal and faithful, most beautiful man I've ever known."

"And you are a stubborn arse who should have re-alized the truth much sooner," Luc sighed in return, arching as best he could into Red's kisses and touch.

Red burst into a laugh, resting his head against Luc's chest for a moment, then lifting his face to grin at Luc. "I know," he said. "But I promise on my honor that I will do my best to only ever match your stub-bornness instead of exceeding it."

It was Luc's turn to laugh at those endearing words. "I can be quite stubborn, you know," he said.

"I most definitely know," Red replied.

He rained a few more kisses across Luc's belly be-fore shifting to a comfortable spot between Luc's legs that wouldn't jostle the splint, then bending down to take the base of Luc's prick in hand. Luc moaned with pleasure that went far deeper than his cock as Red gave him a few strokes, then lowered his mouth to stroke his tongue from his base to tip, licking the moisture that had formed there, then teasing Luc with short kisses and sucks that only took in his flared head.

It felt so good without being quite enough. Luc reached to thread his fingers through Red's hair, grin-ning as he attempted to nudge his lover into taking him deeper. Red resisted, licking and kissing him and driving him mad. Luc used what strength and leverage he had to try to push his hips up and thrust his cock into Red's mouth, but Red pulled back never letting him get very far. It was a sinful game, and Luc had the horrible feeling he would lose.

There was no shame in losing that kind of a game with Red, though. As soon as he gave up with a shudder and relaxed so that Red could have his way with him, whatever that way might be, Red laughed and plunged deep, taking Luc all the way into the heat and wetness of his mouth. It felt so good that Luc's balls drew up in anticipation of orgasm.

"I win," Red murmured between slow, long, deep swallows.

"We both win," Luc gasped in return, tightening his hold on Red's hair.

Red laughed, the vibrations doing amazing things to Luc's cock, then pulled away entirely. He moved over Luc, repositioning himself so that their hips were level and he could fist their cocks together.

"You're right," he said. "We both win."

He bent down to kiss Luc passionately, deftly managing to stroke their cocks even harder as he did. What Red lacked in self-restraint and forbearance he definitely made up for in other areas. Within minutes, he had Luc panting and desperate and teetering on the verge of orgasm. All it took was those few simple words, "I love you, my darling," to have Luc spilling himself with a heartfelt cry of pleasure.

Red was only moments behind him, and he made the most delicious sounds of pleasure and surrender as he milked every last bit from them. Even after the intensity of the moment passed, Luc was left with a burning desire to hold Red close, to kiss him, and to never let him go. They flopped together in an awkward jumble of arms and legs that was as beautiful as it was messy.

"I'm never going to let you go now," Luc told Red, smiling and kissing his cheek as he did.

"I wouldn't want you to," Red answered with a kiss of his own. "We belong together, in everything, and we always will."

I HOPE you've enjoyed Red and Luc's story! War is a terrible thing, and the scars that it leaves us with aren't something that we can get over easily. I've often thought about how the men who fought in wars, like the Napoleonic Wars, long before the recognition of PTSD or survivor's guilt, made the difficult transition to "normal" life after those wars were over. I would like to think that there was some sort of community support that these men could receive, even if the finer points of psychology and trauma were still decade, even centuries, away from being recognized. I think recovery from war is probably one of the factors that contributed to the huge popularity of clubs in the 19th century.

And it wasn't just the war that disrupted lives in the early days of the 19th century either. As Haight and Red discussed, the swift and far-reaching changes of the Industrial Revolution more or less made people's lives unrecognizable within a relatively short amount of time. England was far ahead of the rest of the world when it came to industrialization—which was one of the main contributing factors to the supremacy of the British Empire during the 19th century—but I have to believe that it was also "ahead" in terms of the emotional stress that came with a shift in everything people believed to be true about their way of life. But in the end, industrialization made so much possible.

Take medicine, for example. I had an eye-opening (and cringe-worthy) time researching Regency-era treatments for broken legs while writing this book. 1816 was before many of the advances in medical technology that led to what we think of as modern medicine, but broken bones have been around from the start. What I learned in my research is that breaking a bone was more or less a career-ending injury for most people. The knowledge of how to set and heal broken bones is ancient, but doing so without permanent damage was rare. I also had to give a salute to a real life, famous bonesetter of the 18th century, Sarah "Crazy Sally" Mapp, who was renown throughout England for her bone-setting skills. Medicine was technically a male-dominated profession, but since formal training and licensing wasn't required in England until the Medical Act of 1858, anyone who had a knack for healing, including women, could get away with treating patients.

THERE ARE MORE stories from Wodehouse Abbey on the way! What has been going on between Spencer Brightling and the gamekeeper, Declan Sterling? Could the shy young man be just what wounded Spencer needs to recover from the war? Or will Goddard get in the way in his attempts to seek revenge for the wrongs he imagines have been done to him? Find out next in *Under His Lover's Wing*.

OTHER WORKS BY MERRY FARMER

<u>The Brotherhood – (M/M Victorian Romance)</u>

Just a Little Wickedness

Just a Little Temptation

Just a Little Danger

Just a Little Seduction

Just a Little Heartache

Just a Little Christmas

Just a Little Madness

Just a Little Gamble

Just a Little Mischief

Just a Little Rivalry

<u>The Silver Foxes of Westminster – (M/F Victorian Romance)</u>

December Heart

August Sunrise

May Mistakes

September Awakening

April Seduction

October Revenge

June Forever

<u>The May Flowers – (M/F Victorian with one M/M)</u>

A Lady's First Scandal

It's Only a Scandal if You're Caught

The Scandal of a Perfect Kiss

The Earl's Scandalous Bargain

When Lady Innocent Met Dr. Scandalous

The Road to Scandal is Paved with Wicked Intentions

Scandal Meets Its Match

'Twas the Night Before Scandal

How to Avoid a Scandal (Or Not)

<u>When the Wallflowers were Wicked – (M/F Regency)</u>

The Accidental Mistress

The Incorrigible Courtesan

The Delectable Tart

The Bushing Harlot

The Cheeky Minx

The Clever Strumpet

The Devilish Trollop

The Playful Wanton

The Charming Jezebel

The Faithful Siren

The Holiday Hussy

The Captive Vixen

The Substitute Lover

<u>That Wicked O'Shea Family – (M/F Victorian set in Ireland)</u>

I Kissed an Earl (and I Liked It)

If You Wannabe My Marquess

All About That Duke

Earls Just Wanna Have Fun

All the Single Viscounts

Give Your Heart a Rake

Naughty Earls Need Love Too

And many more! Click here for a complete list of works by
Merry Farmer [http://merryfarmer.net]

ABOUT THE AUTHOR

Merry Farmer lives in suburban Philadelphia with her two cats, Justine and Peter. She has been writing since she was ten years old and realized she didn't have to wait for the teacher to assign a creative writing project to write something. It was the best day of her life. Her books have reached the top of Amazon's charts, and have been named finalists for several prestigious awards, including the RONE Award for indie romance.

9 781648 391446